Cruising for Murder

Stephen E Stanley

Cruising for Murder

Stephen E Stanley
Copyright 2014

ISBN-14 978-1497471030
ISBN-10 1497471036

Printed in the United States of America
Stonefield Publishing 2014

Books by Stephen E Stanley

A MIDCOAST MURDER
A Jesse Ashworth Mystery

MURDER IN THE CHOIR ROOM
A Jesse Ashworth Mystery

THE BIG BOYS DETECTIVE AGENCY
A Jesse Ashworth Mystery

MUDER ON MT. ROYAL
A Jesse Ashworth Mystery

COASTAL MAINE COOKING
The Jesses Ashworth Cook Book

DEAD SANTA!
A Jesses Ashworth Mystery

MURDER AT THE WINDSOR CLUB
A Jeremy Dance Mystery

UP IN FLAMES
A Jeremy Dance Mystery

ALL THE WAY DEAD
A Luke Littlefield Mystery

Characters

Jesse Ashworth- *retired English teacher and co-owner of the Bigg-Boyce Security Agency*

Tim Mallory- *retired chief of the Bath, Maine police department and co-owner if the Bigg-Boyce Security Agency*

Jay Collins-Ashworth- *Jesse's grown son*

Jessica Mallory Cooper- *Tim's daughter and office manager of the security agency*

Derek Cooper- *Bath police officer and occasional detective for the agency. He is Tim's son-in-law*

Rhonda Shepard- *Jesse's best friend, retired teacher, and owner of the Erebus gift shop*

Viola Vickner- *Rhonda's store clerk and Bath's pagan priestess.*

Jason Goulet- *Tim and Jesse's high school classmate and part time security system installer.*

Monica Ashworth Goulet- *Jesse's cousin, married to Jason*

Billy Simpson- *high school classmate of Jesse, Tim, and Jason*

Jackson Bennett- *owner of the largest insurance agency in the mid-coast region and engaged to Rhonda*

Argus- *Jesse's pug dog*

Jake- *Jason's French bulldog.*

Parker Reed- *former captain of the windjammer Doris Dean. First mate of the Prince of Denmark*

Melody Collins- *wants to find out what happened to her brother years ago*

Pierre Hudon- *security chief of the Prince of Denmark*

Brent Dexter- *show manager on the Prince of Denmark and former Morse High School music teacher.*

Author's Note:

This book is a work of fiction. All characters, names, institutions, and situations depicted in the book are the product of my imagination and not based on any persons living or dead. Anyone who thinks he or she is depicted in the book is most likely delusional and should be institutionalized.

Stonefield Publishing
Portland, Maine
StonefieldPublishing@gmail.com

Author's Web page: http://stephenestanley.com/

"Grow old along with me! The best is yet to be, the last of life, for which the first was made. Our times are in his hand who saith, 'A whole I planned, youth shows but half; Trust God: See all, nor be afraid!"

-Robert Browning

Chapter 1

The sun rose slowly and was low in the sky even though it was already seven thirty in the morning. Maine winters tend to be long and cold. I looked out the window and saw the heavy frost on the lawn.

I was alone in bed. Neither my partner Tim Mallory nor my pug dog Argus were anywhere to be found. I propped myself up on the pillows and was reluctant to get out of bed when Tim came through the door carrying a steaming cup of coffee. Argus jumped up on the bed and settled in next to me.

"Happy birthday!" said Tim being way too cheerful for a winter morning.

"Thanks," I replied bleakly.

"How about I take you out for breakfast at Ruby's?"

"Perfect. I'm in the mood for Ruby's ricotta orange pancakes," I said. I like to cook, but I don't cook breakfast. And in case you're wondering, I don't make pie crust and I don't frost cakes, either.

**

I have two ways of looking at birthdays. The first way is that it's a celebration of being alive and having made it to this point. It's a time to celebrate. But the other way I see birthdays is that it's a reminder of the slow march to the grave. It was my birthday and it was a BIG one, too. And I'm afraid that my attitude as I woke up wasn't the optimistic one. If anyone referred to a certain number today they were in danger of being bitch slapped.

The only upside of my birthday was the fact that almost everyone else in my circle of friends was older than I, if only by a few weeks. Tim Mallory, had had his birthday a month ago. My best friend Rhonda Shepard was six years older than I and had no sympathy for my tragic state.

**

"Something the matter Dad?" asked my son Jay. We were working together in the kitchen preparing finger food. Argus was sitting on the floor watching to see if something would fall on the floor.

"Getting old sucks," I complained.

"You're not old," he replied. "You're only…"

"Don't say it."

"…getting better, I was going to say."

"What's going on?" asked my cousin Monica as she poked her head into the kitchen.

"Dad's being a bitch about his birthday."

"Suck it up Jesse," she hissed. "You look amazing for your age."

"That's for sure," said Tim Mallory as he entered the kitchen and hugged me from behind. I relaxed. "All he needs is a hug when he gets cranky."

"What's going on in here?" asked Rhonda Shepard as she leaned into the kitchen pass-through.

"Birthday blues," answered Jay. "Dad, go sit down and relax with your friends. I'll finish up here. You don't need to work on your birthday."

"Let's go old man," said Tim grabbing me and shoving me into the living room. Monica's husband and my best friend, Jason Goulet, passed me a glass of wine. I looked over at Billy Simpson sitting across from me as he drank from a wine glass. "It's only grape juice," he said when he saw me looking at him.

"Of course," I answered. Billy had been sober for almost three years now. I felt guilty for having a momentary doubt.

"Where's Jackson?" I asked Rhonda. Jackson Bennett owned the biggest insurance agency in town and was Rhonda's fiancé.

"He texted me from the office. He said he would meet us at the restaurant."

"You know how to text?" I asked. Rhonda wasn't known for her use of technology.

"Not really," she answered.

Just then a car door slammed and Argus came running out of the kitchen barking along with Jason and Monica's French bulldog Jake. Argus has amazing hearing and can recognize the sound of cars and occupants. From the way Argus was acting I could tell that Tim's daughter Jessica and her husband Derek Cooper had arrived.

"Where's my second favorite dad?" asked Jessica as she came through the door unbuttoning her heavy winter coat. She passed her coat to Derek and ran over and hugged me. "Happy birthday," she said.

"Whatever," I answered.

"I hope I'm in as good a shape when I'm as old as you," said Derek shaking my hand. Everyone laughed.

"This is nice," I admitted as I looked around at a room filled with friends and family.

"Where's Parker?" asked Jason Goulet. Parker Reed is Billy's partner. Parker Reed and I have a history dating back to a summer spent on a Maine windjammer. Parker was then the first mate of the *Doris Dean*, and I was the cook. We shared a cabin that summer and all that implies.

"Parker just reported to a new job down in Boston," sighed Billy.

"What job?" I asked.

Before anyone could answer Tim proposed a toast. "To the birthday boy." Jay passed around the plate of appetizers. Argus jumped onto my lap and licked my face. Maybe my birthday wouldn't be all that bad.

**

The Maine Dining Room at the Harraseeket Inn was crowded, and we had a short wait while they set up our mtable. Jackson Bennett was waiting for us at the bar and we were soon seated.

The inn is my favorite restaurant and since it was my birthday we all got in our cars and drove out to Freeport.

It's always nice to be surrounded with friends and good food on a cold winter's night. There was no snow on the ground yet, but it was bitter cold outside with the temperature hovering around zero.

Everyone had a smug look on their faces, and I didn't know what exactly they were planning. I had threatened to walk out if they had any of the wait staff sing happy birthday. That's okay for someone in their twenties, but at my age it would be embarrassing.

When our drinks arrived we toasted to friendship and then everyone turned to Tim as he produced an envelope from his jacket pocket.

"Happy birthday," he said as he passed it to me.

"Thanks," I replied as I held it up to the light to see if I could guess what was inside. I was confident that it was the L.L. Bean gift certificate I had asked for.

"Open it," said Rhonda as she sipped her glass of white wine.

"Okay," I said as I thought of all the shopping I could do at the store up the street. I tore open the envelope and two tickets fell out. "Concert tickets?" I asked somewhat confused.

"Put your glasses on and read them," said Tim.

I did as I was told and read the tickets out loud. "Copenhagen Cruise lines; Prince of Denmark; February 10 to February 24. Round trip from Boston to the Caribbean. Cabin 8602."

"We're going on a cruise," said Tim with excitement in his voice.

"Us, too," said Rhonda as she held up similar tickets. "We're going, too," said my cousin Monica and Jason nodded his head as confirmation.

"Count me in also," added Billy Simpson.

"I'm not," sighed Jay. "I have to be at school, but I'll be house sitting and keeping poor Argus and Jake company.

"And Derek and I will look after the agency while you guys are gone," added Jessica. The agency she was referring to is the Bigg-Boyce Security Agency that Tim and I own. It's nicknamed The Big Boys' Detective Agency by the locals.

"How did you get this idea?" I asked Tim.

"It was actually Parker Reed who suggested it. He just started a new job as a crew member on the ship." Parker Reed was until recently the skipper of the windjammer *Doris Dean* out of Camden Harbor.

"He's an officer," said Billy Simpson with pride. "The cruise line pays much better than the windjammer's owners." I wasn't surprised since the *Doris Dean* only sail five months out of the year.

"This is the best birthday ever," I said as the waiter arrived to take our orders.

**

Fortunately no singing waiters appeared to sing happy birthday and when we arrived back at Eagle's Nest, the name of the house I bought five years ago, Jay brought out an ice cream cake.

"Tell me about the ship," I said to Billy Simpson.

"Well," he began, "it's the newest ship in the Copenhagen fleet. "It's also one of the largest. There are almost three thousand passengers and the crew adds almost another thousand."

"I got us a balcony cabin," said Tim. "It's one of the best ones."

"It will be great to get away from the cold for a while," added Rhonda. "I know how much you hate winter."

It was true. I hate winter. I love the change of seasons and even early winter I enjoy, but winter stays way too long and is way too cold in Maine. So far this year the snow that fell with each storm hadn't stayed on the ground for too long. That was okay with me, though the skiers were complaining. Too bad for them.

"And the ports we're going to sound great," offered Billy.

"Where are we going, by the way?" I asked.

"It's in here," answered Tim as he held up the cruise line's brochure.

"Who's going to look after the store?" I asked Rhonda. Rhonda is the owner of Bath's premier gift shop Erebus. It was Rhonda's purchase of the gift shop that caused us to end up in Bath, Maine when we both retired from teaching in New Hampshire. I had grown up in Bath and it was good to be back.

"Viola, of course. She'd love to be in charge for a while." Viola Vickner is Rhonda's store clerk and Bath's pagan priestess. She and Rhonda try to outdo each other in outrageous fashions. Viola favors New Age outfits, while Rhonda dresses in vintage attire. Mostly Rhonda wins.

"You'll return and find out that your shop has been turned into a pagan supply store," I said.

"Ha! Half my inventory is already New Age crap."

"Crap?"

"It's a theory," she replied.

"We really hate to leave our baby," sighed my cousin Monica, "but Jay says it will be fun to take care of him and Argus." The baby in question is a French bulldog that they just adopted from a rescue group, named Jake. Argus and Jake get along great.

"That's quite a jump from the *Doris Dean* to the *Prince of Denmark*," remarked Jason to Billy.

"Parker worked on big oil tankers before downsizing to the windjammer fleet. Don't forget that he is a graduate of the Maine Maritime Academy. It's quite an opportunity."

"You won't be seeing much of him then," I said.

"Well here's the other piece of news," he smiled. "I'm going to be working on the ship, too."

"That's great Billy," said Tim. "What are you going to be doing?"

"Well. I've been taking travel agent courses. I was able to get a position with the shore excursion staff of the ship."

"That's wonderful," I said. Billy had come a long way in the last few years. Five years ago Billy was married to his high school girlfriend. He was a sad, hen-pecked husband. After his wife had a psychotic break and was sent to prison, Billy checked himself into rehab, divorced Becky, and met the handsome Parker Reed. Billy is living proof that you can change your life, even if you are looking at middle age in the rear view mirror.

Billy had gotten rid of his middle-age spread and disheveled appearance. Now he was fit and trim, clean shaven, and had short cropped salt and pepper hair and was really quite handsome.

"And here's another surprise," said Billy. "You remember Mr. Dexter our music teacher during senior year?"

We all nodded. Billy, Tim, Jason, and I were in the same graduating class at Morse High. Brent Dexter was a new teacher and only four years older than the senior class at the time. He was good looking and all the senior girls were swooning over him, some of the boys, too, but I'm not naming names.

"He's the entertainment manager on the ship."

"I wonder if he will remember us," remarked Tim.

"Oh, yes," said Billy. "He remembers us."

Chapter 2

Jessica Mallory Cooper as the office manager of the Bigg-Boyce Agency had any new mother's dream job. It wasn't overly demanding, and she was able to bring the baby to work with her. I've seen her nurse the baby, answer the phone, and type out a report all at the same time.

I was in my office trying to work on a packing list. The cruise was in two weeks. Tim and Jason were out setting up a new security system for a little mom and pop convenience store. The store had recently been held up and the owners decided they needed protection. The problem was that neither mom nor pop have any aptitude for technology. This was Tim and Jason's third visit to the site to teach them the system.

"Someone here to see you," announced Jessica as she led the woman into my office.

I stood up and introduced myself and indicated the red chair across from my desk. She told me her name was Melody Collins.

"How can I help you, Mrs. Collins?" Melody Collins looked to be a few years older than I, but she still retained that ageless beauty that some women achieve. She was dressed in a grey business suit with a pink blouse and had her blonde hair tied back in a bun.

"I understand that you're good at finding missing persons."

"We've had some luck along those lines," I said. "Why don't you tell me what it is you need." She sat back in the chair and looked defeated. I could tell by looking at her more closely that she was older than I had first thought. Her manner of dress and the quality of her outfit indicated that she was well off. She hesitated a moment and then a determine look came over her.

"I want you to find out what happened to my brother."

"I see. Maybe you should start at the beginning," I suggested. She nodded and then hesitated as she gathered up her thoughts.

"It was 1953. I was ten years old. My brother John Wilson was sixteen. I adored my brother. I remember the day perfectly. It was May 28 and it was my birthday. My parents had planned a big party for me. Lots of balloons and pony rides; that sort of thing. My brother had just bought a car. It was a 1951 Chevrolet. He and his best friend Dave Wallace went out for a ride. They never came back."

"They never came back? You never heard from him again?" I scribble notes as fast as I could.

"It was like they disappeared off the face of the earth."

"Where was this?"

"We were living in Rockland."

"And your parents contacted the police?"

"Of course. Neither the Rockland police nor the Maine state police turned up anything. It was like they disappeared into thin air."

"This is most unusual," I said. "Usually something turns up after all this time."

"Will you take the case?" she asked.

"You want me to find out what happened to your brother?"

"Yes."

"It may not be possible," I explained. "This is well before credit cards and cell phone records. There's not likely to be any type of trail. And if the police at the time came up with nothing, then it's possible that I'll find zilch." I was about to refuse the case, but the little small voice in my head was urging me to take the case on. Sometimes I hate that voice, but I know that to ignore it is to tempt fate.

"I'll see what I can do," I said. "But I have to warn you we may not be successful."

"I understand."

"Jessica at the front desk will give you the forms and payment schedule."

"Thank you so much," she said with tears welling up.

**

Derek Cooper, Tim, Jason, Jessica and I were sitting in the office break room. Derek had just finished his shift at the Bath Police Department. I was filling them in on the meeting I had with Melody Collins. Derek was holding the sleeping baby. Argus was sitting in my lap pretending to sleep, but he kept one eye open to watch the proceedings.

"1953?" exclaimed Derek. "Everybody from that time period is dead." Tim and I gave him a dirty look. "Sorry," he said.

"Anyway," I continued. "People just don't disappear into thin air. Something happened to those two boys."

"You think they ran away?" asked Jessica.

"It's possible," said Tim. "Back then it would have been much easier to disappear than it is today. They may not have even had their Social Security numbers assigned. Back then you didn't have to have one until you began working."

"I'll check with the sister," I said. "Maybe she'll know if the boys had jobs in high school."

"That's a start," agreed Derek. "If you don't have an answer by the time of your cruise, I'll do the best I can to follow up.

"Hopefully we can wrap this up before the cruise," said Tim. "I don't want to think of work while we're away."

"I think the best place to start is with Black Broker," I said. Black Broker is a deep search engine and data base catalogue developed for government agencies. We were able to buy the security software only because I went to college with the software developer. It was a handy tool, but it didn't solve problems by itself. That being said the Bigg-Boyce Agency had a near perfect record in finding missing persons. So far at least, though I was afraid this case would change that.

"What are your feelings on this?" asked Jessica. They all looked at me. I should explain. I come from a family of Spiritualists and my grandmother was a Spiritualist minister, and my great great grandfather Sebastian Ashworth, was one of the founding members of the Spiritualist movement. Both my cousin Monica and I were trained by my grandmother to believe in intuition. Our parents were not pleased by the way. As adults Monica and I became free thinkers, and we don't believe in talking to the dead. Still there were times when we have very strong feelings about things. If I ignored my gut feelings I did so at my peril.

"The only feelings I have is that we should take the case. Don't ask me why."

"Good enough for me," said Tim. He's had experience with my gut feelings in the past and has learned to go along with them. "Hopefully we can wrap this up before we go on the cruise."

"Hopefully," I agreed, though I wasn't getting a feeling one way or another.

**

Back in my office I fed the names Dave Wallace and John Wilson into Black Broker along with the date 1953, the location of Rockland, Maine. Black Broker is very thorough in its search, but it takes a few hours to come up with a detailed report. In the mean time I picked up the phone and called Monica.

"I was just going to call you," she said by way of greeting.

"How about meeting me for coffee in half an hour at the coffee shop?

"Okay," she answered. "See you there."

＊＊

I was relieved to see that Brian Stillwater was working the coffee bar and not Judy Blair. Judy Blair was given the nickname Bitch Blair back in high school for a reason. Brian made me a nice latte, and I took a seat in the corner while Monica waited for her espresso.

"What case are you working on now?" she asked.

"How did you know that I wanted to talk to you about a case?"

She just shrugged her shoulders. I gave her an outline of the case. "I agree with you," she said after I told her the facts, "you were meant to take the case."

"That was my feeling," I said. "But I don't really know why."

"If they are still alive they will be seventy-eight years old."

"And been missing for sixty-two years."

"This case will be a real challenge for you and Tim," she said as she sipped on her espresso.

"The trouble is I don't know where to start."

"Isn't your super computer program going to help?"

"Maybe, but we're looking back at a time before digital records. The search process can only search for information that exists. 1953 was a very primitive time period if you look at record keeping."

"They had computers back then didn't they?"

"They had Univac; it was about the size of a house and could only do basic calculations. Your smart phone has one hundred times the computing power. We won't find any help in that direction."

"How's Jay getting along?" she asked to change the subject. Jay is my son. Until two years ago I didn't know he existed. Now I can't imagine my life without him. Like me he became an English teacher. When he finally tracked me down I convinced him to move to Bath to be near me. It's been wonderful.

"He loves teaching at Morse High, he made some good friends, and he's saving to buy a house."

"No boyfriend in the picture?"

"I don't think so. Teaching takes a lot of energy. Sometimes there's not much left over."

"I guess. Look at you. You didn't find Tim until after you retired."

"And you should talk. You dumped Jerry Twist when your kids were grown and found Jason Goulet. My cousin marrying my best friend."

"There is joy in the second half of life," said Monica with a smile.

"That's for sure," I said.

Chapter 3

When I returned back to work Black Broker had spit out some information for me to sift through. I eliminated all the Dave Wallaces and John Wilsons who didn't fit the time period. There was a lot of information to cull. Finally I got to the link for the news story from the *Portland Press Herald*.

Search On For Missing Teenagers
(Rockland) Two teenagers, both age 16, have been reported missing according to Rockland police. David Wallace and John Wilson, both of Rockland, were last seen on Thursday morning when they set out in Wilson's dark green 1951 Chevy coupe to visit friends in Camden. They never arrived. Wallace is 5'9" with brown wavy hair and Wilson is 5' 10" with a blond crew cut. The plate number of the Chevy is 423-112. Anyone with any information is asked to contact the Rockland police.

The news story was useful in that it gave an idea on where to go from here. It might be a good idea to talk to the two friends in Camden. That is if I can find them and if they are still alive. I put a call into Melody Collins to see if she remembered the names of her brother's two friends. She didn't remember. So far I had learned only what I already knew: that two sixteen year old boys went missing in 1953.

"What's for dinner?" asked Tim poking his head into my office.

"What?" I asked.

"Dinner; it's quitting time."

I looked at the clock. "So it is. I need to go to the store. You take Argus and I'll meet you at home." Argus heard his name and came out from under my desk where he was napping.

"Forget about dinner did you?" asked Tim smiling.

"No. we're having chicken pie," I replied making it up on the spot. I like to keep him guessing. The truth was I hadn't given dinner a thought.

Tim left with Argus, and I got into my car and headed to the store to pick up the needed ingredients.

When I got home Tim had a chilled glass of white wine waiting for me. "I know that look," he said. "What's on your mind?"

"I'm not sure why I took this case. How are we ever going to unravel a sixty year old mystery?" I told him about my plan to interview Wilson's two friends in Camden if I could find them, but Melody couldn't remember their names.

"That's easy," said Tim, the ex-cop. "Their names are going to be in the police report. The police would have interviewed them and it's got to be in their report."

"I knew I kept you around for a reason," I said as I relaxed and headed to the kitchen. "I should start dinner." I went into the kitchen and made a meal. Frozen mixed vegetables, cooked chicken, cream of chicken soup, and biscuit mix and dinner was in the oven.

The phone rang and Tim answered it. "It's for you," he said as he handed me the phone.

"How the hell am I going to pack for a two week cruise?" yelled Rhonda on the other end. Clearly she was having an anxiety attack.

"It's simple," I replied. "Place everything you need in a suitcase and close the cover."

"Asshole!"

"You've got two weeks to plan," I said reasonably. "It's the Caribbean. The temperature is going to be in the eighties. Shorts, sandals, and top. Dressy casual for dinner most nights and something nice for formal nights. You can have them do your laundry, so don't worry. Just remember, you pack it, you carry it."

"I suppose you're all packed?"

"I haven't even thought about it yet. Tim and I have a case to work on." I told her about the missing boys.

"Sixty years ago? What can you do that the police couldn't do?"

"We have record keeping and digital footprints these days. It's harder to go off the grid now. If they're still alive we might be able to track them down."

"And if they're dead?"

19

"Then it's going to be a hell of a lot harder," I replied. "I haven't talked to the dead in a long time."

**

Black Broker had spit out some additional results for me to look at as I entered my office the next morning. I was getting better at sifting through results. The one down side to the computer program was that it was sometimes too thorough, coming up with pages of results. I was learning how to narrow searches to eliminate extraneous information. The program produced a follow up article in the local newspaper. There didn't seem to be much additional information.

Search Continues for Missing Teens

(Rockland) The search continues for two missing teens, David Wallace and John Wilson, both 16. The boys were last seen leaving the Wilson home of May 28th. It was reported by the family that the boys were planning to visit friends in Camden, but never arrived. A search of the area has revealed no clues. A search of the nearby quarries turned up nothing. Police have not ruled out foul play.

I read and reread the article, and I had a few
questions. What type of search did they do and how
thorough was the search? Did they assume that the boys
had run off? I would have to make a trip to Rockland and
check the police record. I'd take Tim with me. As an ex-
cop, the police were more likely to share information
with him than with me.

I walked into Tim's office with Argus close at my
heels. Tim was seated at his desk and Argus went to him
and jumped onto his lap. Whenever Argus sees an empty
lap, he feels it's his duty to fill it. "Any luck with Black
Broker?" he asked stroking the dog's coat.

"All I came up with were two newspaper articles
which pretty much confirms what we already know. I
can't locate the names of his two friends the boys were
planning to visit. It must be in the police report as you
suggested. I thought we could take a ride to Rockland and
check the records."

"If we leave now we can be at Moody's Diner by
lunch time." Moody's Diner is a Maine institution.
Located in Waldoboro, Maine, on Route One it opened
up in 1934 to take advantage of the new automobile
traffic that was beginning to increase along the coast.
Homemade food has been the hallmark for over eighty
years.

"Let's go," I said. Argus heard the word go and began
dancing and barking.

"We can't take Argus and leave him in the car, even
if it is winter."

"I'll call Viola and see if she can dog sit."

"Is she working at Erebus today?"

"I think she might be off, but I'll give her a call." I called Viola at home, and she was more than willing to dog sit. Viola is one of those people to whom animals flock. Argus would have a fun day. We both decided to drive out to Viola's and then hit Route One to Rockland. We drove out to North Bath to Viola's mobile home. We cruised up through the north end of town until we hit Whiskeag Road. It used to be a fun ride with its bumps and turns until a few years ago when the highway department graded the road.

"I miss Granny's Tickle," I sighed. Granny's Tickle was the name that locals gave one of the larger bumps in the road. If you drove at just the right speed, your car would become air born for a few seconds.

"I think there were too many accidents when people went too fast."

"That's because people don't know how to drive anymore."

"Someone," said Tim, "is sounding like an old man."

"I need to point out that you are older than I," I replied. We pulled into Viola's driveway, and she threw on a jacket and came out to greet us. Argus flew out of the car and jumped into Viola's arms. Viola's lot of land was always interesting. As the local pagan priestess, she made her yard reflect her beliefs. There were rock cairns situated in the four corners of the lot for the elemental spirits. A small, faceless, statue of the goddess had center place by her front door. Colorful banners hung from the tree branches.

"Bright Blessings! Would you like to come in for some herb tea?" she asked.

"Thanks, but we should get going. Thanks for doing this."

"I love Argus. Take your time; we're going to have a good day. Where are you off to?"

I gave her a brief description of our search. She nodded and said she would light a candle for our success. I figured it couldn't hurt.

"Strange woman," said Tim as we drove away. "But I like her."

"She's a good soul," I agreed. "And I don't think her religion is as hurtful as some I could name."

"It's when religions become too centralized that corruption sets in." I had once been an Episcopalian, but the creeping in of clericalism had sent me running for the door. I like to be a participant, not just a viewer. The obscene amount of money spent on flying bishops to meetings would have been better spent on the poor and hungry. That's just my opinion; I could be wrong.

"All Souls," said Tim, "is a good example of what church should be." All Souls Church was Bath's liberal religious community, and the social center for much of the community, as well as a beacon for social justice. Tim and I were members, and I sang in the choir.

"Anyway," I said changing the subject, "I hope we can find the missing boys." I was suddenly hit with a vision for just a second, but then it was gone. Something was spinning around in my head. I just hoped it would stop long enough for me to look at it.

Chapter 4

Benjamin Nickerson, Rockland's chief of police, ushered us into his office. Ben and Tim knew each other quite well, since Tim used to be Bath's chief of police. "Tim, it's good to see you again," Nickerson said shaking his hand. "And this must be Jesse. I've heard a lot about you."

"Same here," I said shaking his hand. Exactly what he had heard about me I wasn't sure and sometimes it was better not to ask.

"I understand the family has hired you to look into the case. It's still an open case for us but of course…"

"I understand," interrupted Tim. "No small police department has the type of man power to investigate all the unsolved crimes in their files."

"I've made copies of all the reports for you. Could I offer you coffee?"

"That would be great," I said. Tim nodded, too. The chief poured us both a cup of coffee. "Anything you can add that's not in the files?"

"Well," said the chief hesitating, "some of the older officers remember a rumor that it could have been foul play. But you know how rumors are."

"But there was no evidence of that, was there?" asked Tim.

"That's just it. There was no evidence of anything at all."

"Are any of the officers who worked the case still alive?" I asked.

"I doubt it," said the chief shaking his head. "That was a long time ago. If they were in their thirties back in 1953, and most of them were WWII soldiers, then they would be in their late nineties now. And as you know," he said looking at Tim, "policemen don't live too long after retirement."

"What?" I asked. I had never heard of this.

"The average police officer dies within five years of retirement and has a life span some twelve years less than other Americans," the chief said.

"That's true," said Tim.

"Oh, great," I sighed. "One more thing to worry about." Tim has been retired for three years already. Tim saw the look I gave him.

"That's why I didn't retire," said Tim. "I just changed jobs."

"How is business, by the way?" asked Nickerson. "I've always wondered what it would be like to be a private investigator."

"It's great," replied Tim, "unless you are looking for a steady paycheck. Fortunately the security part of the business covers expenses, and we have our pensions to pay for food and shelter, so we can take cases that interest us."

"And you took this case on?" the chief asked.

"Well," I said. "You have to admit that it is challenging." I didn't bother to tell him that a little voice in my head told me I should take the case. Policemen have their own views about people who hear voices.

"Okay," said the chief. "If I can be of any help, let me know. I grew up here, so I know the area quite well."

"You know," I said to Tim when we got back to the car, "he thinks we're crazy."

"I'm not sure that I don't agree with him," said Tim as he put the car into gear.

**

We drove to Camden for a leisurely lunch on the waterfront after we decided that Moody's Diner was too crowded for a relaxing break. Camden bills itself as the prettiest town in Maine, and they have a reason to brag. The small downtown looks the same as it did a hundred years ago and the small harbor, filled with yachts of all sizes, has a range of small mountains as a backdrop.

In winter the windjammers are covered with shrink wrap and small ice flows surround the yachts, but even in February, the town is pretty.

We took a seat near a window of the Harbor View Restaurant. I ordered a steaming bowl of lobster stew. And Tim had a bowl of clam chowder. Nothing to my mind makes a better lunch than beer and chowder.

After lunch we sat with coffee, and I began to look at the files chief Nickerson made for us. The file was many pages long and as I finished reading each page I passed them to Tim. Tim, I knew, with his police background might be able to see things I missed.

"What are you seeing that I missed?" I asked as I handed Tim the last page.

"While it doesn't say so outright, there is the suspicion that there might be foul play."

"How so?" I asked. I hadn't seen any reference to foul play. It seemed like just a missing persons' case to me.

"All the family members and the two Camden friends were asked to confirm their whereabouts during the time of the disappearance."

"Wouldn't that be routine?" I asked.

"Not really. Remember that this is a small town in 1953. The most logical conclusion would be to treat the boys as possible runaways or accident victims. Foul play would be looked into only after some time had passed. But right from the start the investigators looked into the possibility of foul play."

"So there was something going on that doesn't show up in the report?"

"Only facts are in the report, so yes there is more to this case than just the facts."

I was about to say something when Tim's cell phone rang. As he talked he took out the notepad he always carried with him and jotted down whatever information he was being given. After he hung up, he turned to me. "You might want to call Viola and ask if she can dog sit for another day. I think we'll be spending the night here."

**

The Cold Harbor Inn had a discrete rainbow flag at the front door, so we knew we would be welcome. The innkeepers, Joanne and Beth, were friends of mine from way back. Years ago I had worked for them when they ran a bed and breakfast back in Provincetown.

"Jesse, it's so good to see you. It's been what? Twenty years?" asked Beth as she gave me a big bear hug.

"Closer to thirty, I think. It was the 1980s," added Joanne who hugged me next.

"Good times," I said.

"And this strapping hunk is Tim?" asked Beth.

"You got yourself a pretty one," exclaimed Joanne. "But then you always did, didn't you?"

"They used to try and fix me up back when I worked for them," I said.

"No one was ever good enough," said Beth. "Now I know why."

"I think there's a story here," said Tim.

"A story for another time," I said hoping we could drop the subject. There are some things in my past I'd rather not remember.

We were shown to a large room with a fireplace and two overstuffed chairs and a private bath. There were five other similar rooms and even in midwinter the inn was full.

"How is it you're full this time of year?" I asked the two ladies.

"The Camden Snow Bowl offers skiing, and accommodations and food are much cheaper off season."

"This is nice," I said looking around. "I wouldn't mind staying here for a while."

"Maybe we can arrange that," said Tim. "If only we could bring the dog."

"Of course you can bring the dog," said Beth.

"We love dogs," added Joanne. "You remember Scamp?"

"Yes," I said. "I loved Scamp." Scamp was their German shepherd. A sweet-natured dog that used to tag along with me when I went out for walks back in Provincetown.

"Now we have Spike," added Beth. "You'll see him hanging around. He's a pug."

"A Pug? My Argus is a pug."

"Then you have to bring him with you next time," said Joanne. "We insist."

"So are you here for vacation?" asked Beth.

I explained as best I could that we now owned a detective agency in Bath and that we were working on a case. It seemed like we had a lot to get caught up on.

Sitting by the fire in our room, we were again going over the police report from 1953. Much of the report was hand written, and I confess it was hard to read. No one had bothered to have the reports typed out.

"What are the chances we can find the two friends after all these years?" I asked.

"Well, the only way we'll know for sure is to try. Let's start low tech and try the phone book. If that doesn't work we'll have Jessica do a search on Black Broker." Black Broker is a memory hungry software program that won't fit on a mere laptop.

"Ernest St. Claire and Arthur Laski are the names of the two friends," I read aloud while Tim jotted down the names.

"Not all that common," said Tim as he picked up his laptop. He grabbed his cell phone and typed in the names. After a few seconds Tim spoke. "I found one."

"Which one was that?" I asked.

"Ernest St Claire," he said. "Nothing here for Arthur Laski." Tim picked up the phone and placed a call to Jessica, giving her the names to search in Black Broker.

"Well," I said, "it seems that we have the rest of the afternoon free. I wonder what we can do to pass the time?"

"I have a few ideas," said Tim with a look I had come to know quite well.

Chapter 5

During the late afternoon the wind picked up and the temperature dropped to a bitter cold nine degrees Fahrenheit. It was just past five in the afternoon, and it was already dark. Tim and I bundled up and headed out into the cold to walk to a nearby restaurant.

Even with several layers of clothing and an arctic parker I was cold. Tim having years of experience as a police officer had a better tolerance for extremes of weather.

It was less than a ten minute walk to the restaurant, but it took me a full five minutes to warm up once we were seated. We had a good view of the lights of the harbor from where we sat, but I could feel the cold radiating from the window.

I ordered a hot toddy and a cup of steaming clam chowder as a starter, and Tim did the same. I could hear Tim's phone vibrate with a text message. He picked it up and read the message.

"It's from Jessica. According to what she got from Black Broker, Arthur Laski died in 1994. Ernest St. Claire is still alive and lives with his daughter here in Camden. Jessica gave us the address and phone number." Tim called the daughter's number and made arrangements to meet with Ernest St. Claire in the morning.

"I hope he can give us something to go on," I said as I took a sip of the hot toddy. I was beginning to thaw out.

"Anything will be better than what we have now, which is zero," said Tim as our chowder arrived.

I tasted the chowder. It was warm and it was good, and I was feeling much better about being out in the winter weather. "What do you think happened to the boys?" I asked Tim.

"In my experience most teenagers are either runaways or abductees. Either way it's not always a happy ending. What's unusual about this case is that the car was never recovered. Usually an abandoned car will turn up somewhere. But where is the car?"

"Could they have just kept the car? Could they have driven it to California for example, and sold it?"

"It's possible if they had the title with them. Or they could have sold it for parts. Vehicle Identification Numbers did not come into use until 1954 and they weren't standardized until 1981. They disappeared in 1953 and the car was a 1951 model, so there would be no way to track the car that way."

The waitress appeared and we gave our orders for the entrées. Not being able to make up my mind on either scallops or clams, I ordered the seafood platter. Tim ordered the shrimp platter.

"What do you think happened to them?" asked Tim. He was referring to my family gift of intuition.

"That's the strange thing about this," I replied. "I usually have some type of feeling about a case. Usually just enough to get started. I'm getting nothing on this one, which just goes to show you that this psychic crap is a lot of hooey."

"I don't believe that for a moment," said Tim. "I've seen you and Monica come up with some amazing things. I don't know how it works; but it does."

The next morning broke to a red sky and a cold wind. The sunrise was beautiful as it was reflected off the water. Beth and Joanne provided a great breakfast of eggs, ham, hash browns and homemade muffins. Even after all these years they remembered that I loved their cranberry muffins. A storm was predicted to hit the coast later in the morning, and we made arrangements to stay another night rather than try to drive back to Bath in the storm.

"We should be able to walk over to see St. Claire," I said. "Chestnut Street is only a five minute walk."

"No sense starting up the car for a short distance like that."

"And it's beginning to snow," I said as I looked out the window. The snow was coming down in small, light flakes.

We finished our second cup of coffee and then bundled up against the chilling cold. The snow was being blown around by the wind and had not yet settled on the ground. The snow felt like ice pellets as it hit my face.

Ernest St. Claire's house was an early 1900s gingerbread affair that was popular during Camden's boom times. We rang the doorbell, which was a mechanical affair that was most likely original to the house. St. Claire's daughter greeted us at the door and led us into a small parlor where Ernest sat in a large easy chair reading the morning paper and covered with a colorful knitted afghan.

"You must be the detectives," he said as he motioned us to sit down on the sofa.

"I'm Tim Mallory and this is Jesse Ashworth," said Tim. "We just wanted to hear anything you remember about the time the boys disappeared."

"Seems like only yesterday. Time sure passes quickly."

"Maybe you can start by telling us about the boys," I suggested.

"Art, Dave, John and I were best friends. We always hung out together. We were supposed to go up to the lake to fish that day."

"How is it that two Camden boys and two Rockland boys were friends?" asked Tim. Neighboring towns were often bitter high school rivals.

"The four of us worked on a state road crew during the summer clearing brush from the side of the state roads. It was hard work and I guess we bonded," said Ernest.

"Anything unusual about their behavior before they disappeared?" I asked.

"How do you mean?"

"Did they act secretive or strange in any way?" Ernest sat back in his chair and thought about it for a minute or two before he spoke.

"Not really. They talked all summer about going to California someday. But they didn't have enough money to get to Bangor let alone California."

"So tell us about the day they disappeared," suggested Tim. "How did you plan to meet? Did you talk to them over the phone?"

"No we had planned it a few days earlier when we were together. Neither Art nor I had a car and my family didn't have a phone. They never showed up. I knew John's sister was having a birthday, so Art and I figured they stayed for the party. It wasn't until the state police showed up two days later that we learned they were missing."

A sudden thought just occurred to me. "What route did they usually take from Rockland?" I asked.

"I'm almost positive that they always came to Camden on the Old County Road. Of course back then it was just called the County Road. It was more direct to my house than Route One was."

"Anything else you can think of?" asked Tim.

"Nope. Like I said we didn't even know about it until two days later."

"Well," said Tim passing him our business card, "if you think of anything, let us know."

**

Back in the car I said to Tim, "I think we should take a look at Old County Road. If they were really going to Camden, then they must have disappeared somewhere along the road."

"If they really were going to Camden," added Tim. "Remember the fishing day was planned several days before. Maybe they changed their minds and headed out of town in a different direction."

"True," I agreed, "but the sister claims that they were going off to Camden."

"And teenagers often tell their parents they are going one place when they are really planning to go somewhere else." Tim smiled. "If I remember correctly when we were their age we told our parents we were spending a few days at Jason's camp up north and ended up at a rock festival in New York State."

"Good times," I sighed.

"Yes, but we didn't think about the consequences if something had gone wrong."

"True," I said as I headed the car toward Rockland. "But I have a feeling..."

"God help us," interrupted Tim.

I turned the car radio on to the local station. Interestingly enough it was a syndicated show by Stephanie Moonstone, America's foremost radio psychic. I quickly turned the radio off.

"So tell me how it works," asked Tim.

"How what works?" I asked.

"This psychic thing."

"Stephanie Moonstone is a fake," I said.

"Really?"

"Well," I hesitated. "I think she has some gift. But I don't think she's one hundred percent honest. If you listen carefully, you can hear her lead the questioning."

"Your family were psychics weren't they?"

"They were mediums. They belonged to the Spiritualist Church. They had some psychic ability, but really there is no such thing as being able to tell the future."

"No?"

"No. Despite the last five hundred years of Protestant belief in predestination, there is no such thing. The future is fluid, not fixed. We humans have our own version of chaos theory."

"But some psychics are correct about eighty percent of the time."

"You've been doing some reading, haven't you?"

"Yes. I've seen you and Monica at work. So why are they right some eighty percent of the time and not ninety percent or one hundred percent?"

"Okay," I said. "It's like this; people with good intuition," I emphasized the word intuition because I think psychic is an overused and inaccurate term, "are like someone standing on a hill with a view that goes further than a person on the ground. I can see that you are boarding a train and I know that the train is heading to Boston. Therefore I can conclude that you are going to Boston. However you have free will. You can choose to get off the train at any stop along the way. Or someone can ram a truck into the train along the way, or a tornado could pick up the train and hurl it off the tracks. That's chaos theory. So if I told you that you were going to Boston I was correct that you were heading that way, but wrong because for a number of reasons you never made it."

"So you think that no one can tell the future?"

"That's exactly what I think," I said.

"Can they tell the past?"

"That's a different question," I replied. "You only get one metaphysical question a month." I slowed the car down and turned at the sign of the Old County road.

Chapter 6

Route One from Camden had been thickly lined with houses and businesses, but in Rockport when we turned onto the Old County Road the area quickly turned residential and somewhat rural.

"You know," I said, "these houses all seem fairly new considering that this is supposed to be an old road."

"It seems a little too straight too," observed Tim.

"Maybe we should get a map and check out what the road looked like in 1953. It could have been straightened." Just as I said that we turned a corner and the road became more serpentine and dotted with old farm houses.

"Well, this part seems old enough," said Tim. "What are you looking for?"

"I have no idea," I confessed. "I just want to see what the area is like." Looking around all I saw was a bare landscape. All the trees had lost their leaves and even with a layer of snow from yesterday's storm everything looked barren. Here and there were rock piles that seemed to be out of place. It was then that I remembered that this area was a major limestone deposit and that nearby Thomaston still had a cement plant. As we traveled along the road it seemed to straighten out and appeared to be a newer section.

"Stop the car," said Tim. I slammed on the brakes not knowing why he wanted to stop.

"What's wrong?"

"Nothing's wrong." He replied. "tell me what you see."

I looked out the car window and saw a small field overgrown with brush and evergreens. There were piles of rocks off in the distance. "All I see is some brush and evergreens."

"Look again at the flat areas."

It took me a few moments to see what he saw. The flat area of the land was long and narrow and aligned perfectly with the road we were now on. "That's the old road, I'll bet. The road we're on now is new and straighter."

"By the growth of the trees here, I'll bet this was the road as it was back in the fifties," Tim got out of the car and I followed. The snow was about two inches on the ground. I had my L.L. Bean shoes on, the ones with rubber bottoms and leather tops so my feet would stay dry. I hate wet feet.

"I'll bet there's a quarry somewhere in this area. That would account for all the rock piles."

"I don't think this area has been mined since the Civil War. All the mining now takes place in Thomaston."

"Even Camden has quarries," I added. "They used to use one for the town dump. All that debris floating on the top of the water. Just imagine what they would find at the bottom."

"Probably the bodies of missing wives or husbands."

"Are you thinking what I'm thinking?" I asked.

"Let's follow the old road and see."

We were less than a quarter mile away when we saw it. There were old and weather-worn danger signs up along the woods, but time and weather had faded them. Along the side of the old road was a large quarry. It looked deep. About fifty feet down the hole was the ice covered water. It was hard to tell how deep the quarry was, but it was a good guess that it was very deep.

"According to the police report, they checked the area quarries and didn't see evidence of a car going off the road," I said.

"The road is close to the quarry but they would have had guard rails and fences along here." In fact we could see the remainders of the old heavy duty cable guards and wooden posts that used to be along the Maine roads.

"Yes, they would have noticed if the guard rails had been breached." But something in my head was telling me to look around. As I said before I always get into big time trouble if I ignore my gut feeling. I looked down the old abandoned road and then I saw it.

"Look over there Tim. See that slight bump in the road?"

"Yes."

"It's just like another granny's tickle. Just like out on Whiskeag road. I'll bet if you hit it just at the right speed the car will be air born. I'll bet if you were speeding along this road and hit that bump something would happen."

"It might have been just enough for the car to sail over the guard rail and not leave any damage."

I looked down into the darkness of the iced over quarry and shivered.

**

Argus ran out to greet me when we pulled into Viola's driveway. Viola came out and ushered us into her house.

"Thanks for taking care of the little guy," I said as she poured us a cup of herb tea.

"He's been a joy to have around. He follows me from room to room. I'm never alone."

"Especially in the kitchen," added Tim with a laugh.

"How did your trip go?" she asked.

"Jesse here figured out what happened to the two kids we were looking for."

"So you found them?"

"Not yet," I answered. I told her about what I think happened to them. "The state police have a new sophisticated sonar device that they plan on using in the quarry. It will take them a few days to get set up, break the ice, and check the quarry. They'll let us know if they find anything."

"Those poor kids," she said with a sniffle. "But it will be a blessing to put them to rest. You really think they are down there?"

"Yes," I answered. Tim muttered something under his breath that sounded like "scary." I looked at him and shook my head. "I'm not saying anything to the sister until we know for sure."

"Are you excited about your trip?" she asked to change the subject.

"We haven't had much time to think about it," said Tim. "It's only a week away."

"Time to make a packing list, I guess," I added.

"Rhonda's been driving me crazy talking about what clothes she'll need for the cruise. She said she has to go out and get a whole new wardrobe."

"And you're surprised by this?" I asked.

"I'll be surprised if she can fit it all into a suitcase."

"Well," said Tim, "we really should get home. Again thanks for looking after the little guy," he said as he scooped Argus up in his arms.

"I don't think I have anything for dinner in the house," I said as I slipped behind the wheel.

"Wong Ho's?" asked Tim referring to the local Chinese restaurant.

"Let's stop for take-out. I really just want to get home, build a fire, and sit in my chair with a book, and have my guys nearby."

"You saw something when you looked into the quarry, didn't you?"

"It could just be my imagination," I said. The vision I had of a car lying upside down in the water was disturbing.

"I doubt it," said Tim as he reached over and tussled my hair.

**

It was Saturday night and in Maine that means baked beans, ham, and cornbread. I was able to find a farm that grew Jacob's Cattle beans, which are the best baking beans in the world. Even though the bean pot had given way to the crock pot long ago, the cooking still sends the smell of baking beans throughout the house.

The temperature outside had dipped below freezing, and I had a good fire going in the parlor stove. The flickering flames through the glass doors cast a soft glow in the living room. Jay was coming over for supper, along with Jessica and Derek, and the baby. I was looking forward to a family gathering.

Once everyone arrived Tim broke out a bottle of white wine. I brought out shrimp cocktail and we all gathered by the fire.

"Excited about your trip?" asked Jay.

"Not yet," I replied. "I haven't given it much thought yet. I'll be excited as soon as I'm on board, I'm sure. Thanks for taking care of Argus. I'd hate to leave him otherwise, but since you'll be staying here, he probably won't even miss me."

"Oh, he'll miss you alright, but I'll keep him too busy to notice."

Just then the phone rang. Tim picked it up and listened. "I see," I heard him say. "When? We'll be there."

I looked at him and he nodded. "That was my friend Jeff Greenlaw of the state police. They found something on the sonar at the quarry and it looks like a car at the bottom. They're going to try and recover it on Monday, if they can get the equipment down to the site. We should be there.

I just sat down and buried my face in my hands.

Chapter 7

A frigid wind had blown up from Penobscot Bay and the wind chill factor was around zero. Just how far below zero I didn't even want to know. A crowd had gathered by the quarry. A large crane had been set up for the recovery. Melody Collins had insisted on coming and she, Tim, and I were standing with the state police chaplain. The Maine Fish and Game Service is technically in charge of Maine's bodies of water, and they had a full contingent of officers present. There were TV and newspaper reporters, and the story had gone national because it was a sixty year old mystery and made good copy.

Despite the state police's attempt to keep the location quiet, it didn't take locals long to figure out which quarry was the center of action. The transportation of a huge crane along the normally quiet roads was a tip off.

Ice was going to be a major factor in the recovery. It had been mostly a mild winter, but still the water was glazed over with a sheet of ice. The ice was too thin to walk on, but thick enough that it took the recovery team two hours to break it up.

Just watching the divers enter the frigid water made me shiver. I'm sure their suits keep them warm, but it couldn't be pleasant to be submerged in the dark, cold water. The dive team took large hooks connected to cables with them as they disappeared under the surface.

They would somehow have to attach the cables to the car so that the crane could lift it out of the water.

A woman with a microphone and a camera crew started to head our way. I recognized her as a network reporter for the national news. Tim quickly whispered to his state trooper friend and two troopers headed her way and intercepted her. I didn't think Melody needed to give an interview at this point.

A fish and game camper truck rolled up and we went inside where hot coffee and doughnuts were served. Melody looked grim, but I thought her brave to be here; I'm not sure if I could do it if I were in her place. The chaplain hadn't left Melody's side since the beginning, but she must have seen the look on my face because the chaplain came over to me.

"I know this is hard for everyone, but you've done a good thing," she said to Tim and me.

"It seems like we've just brought a lot of pain," I sighed.

"You've brought closure. That's the real gift here."

"Something's happening," said Tim looking out of the camper's window. We went outside and stood by the rim of the quarry. They were pulling out the four divers and they ushered them into another camper. The cable on the crane tightened and very slowly began to lift up the large object on the bottom.

"Maybe it's just someone's abandoned junk car, I heard one of the troopers say. I knew it wasn't. I knew it was a 1951 Chevy, and I knew there would be two remains of skeletons in the wreck.

It seemed to take forever before we sighted the wreck as it got close to the surface. Water poured out of the rusted wreck as it slowly broke the surface of the water. Once the wreck was clear of the surface the crane stopped until the water drained out of it. Even in its rusted state it was clear that it was an older model car. The car swung around on the cable making the scene even more eerie if that was possible.

It would be several days before an official statement would come out that the case of two missing Rockland teenagers who disappeared in 1953 had been solved.

**

Tim and I were in the small conference room at the office making up a "to do" list for Derek and Jessica who would be running the agency while we were away. We both knew they were more than capable of running the business for a few weeks, but it made us feel better to make up the list. Jay would be house sitting at Eagle's Nest with Argus and Jake, and I had made sure to put the vet's phone number on the refrigerator door.

Jessica came and stood in the doorway, "Melody Collins is here to settle up the bill."

"Send her in," said Tim. She entered and I indicated that she should take a seat at the table with us. Jessica passed me a folder with the expense report and contracted billable hours.

"I'm sure you've heard," she said. "But the forensic report came back that positively identified the skulls as belonging to my brother and his friend."

"Yes, we've heard," I answered. In fact it had been broadcast on almost every national news outlet. Though the major facts of the story focused on the recovery, our part in the case was mentioned and I was confident that business would pick up for the Bigg-Boyce Security Agency.

I passed the folder to Tim. He looked inside, made a note and then passed it back to me. I read the note, took out the contract and wrote "paid in full" on it and gave it to Melody.

"I don't understand," she said.

"The publicity of this case will more than pay for our expenses," I said. "It is an honor to be able to give closure to the families. This has been very painful for you and we are not taking your money."

Melody looked at us and burst into tears.

Chapter 8

It was a sunny winter day with the temperatures hovering in the forties when we all set out on our cruise adventure. Tim, Jason, Monica and I piled into my car and headed to the train station in Portland. Rhonda and Jackson took their own car and would meet us there. Billy and Parker had already started their jobs on the new ship. We were staying in a Boston hotel for the night and then boarding the ship in the morning.

Our hotel was in the financial district of the city. It was a business hotel during the week, and more or less tourist accommodations on the week end. We all checked in and went out for a late lunch at the No Name Restaurant. The No Name is about as unpretentious as you can get. Located on Boston's fish pier, it was first opened in 1917. As an avowed seafood lover I can attest to the seafood chowder. We found a table and we all ordered the seafood platter.

"I'm excited," said Rhonda. "This will be my first cruise. What's the ship like?"

"According to Billy," replied Tim, "it's a mega ship. It holds over three thousand passengers, has about ten restaurants, and two pools plus a water slide."

"You know," I said, "I think we need to celebrate. Look at us all. At a time when most people retire and collect their pensions, we've all started second careers."

"Yes, indeed," said Rhonda. "Though we all are collecting our pensions as well."

"Which allows us now to work for fun and not profit," I replied.

"I'm especially proud of Billy," broke in Tim. "Here is someone who in the course of the last three years has totally turned his life around."

"And look at Parker. Imagine going from a small windjammer to a giant cruise ship," said Monica.

"Remember he was a captain of an oil tanker before the windjammer. But still that was a long time ago." My mind drifted back to the summers spent working with him on the windjammer *Doris Dean*.

**

The Black Falcon Cruise Terminal on Boston's waterfront had undergone a recent renovation, and despite the confluence of disembarking passengers and arriving cruisers, check in was easy. Once we started making our way up to the ship on the glassed in gang plank, we got to really take in the size of the ship.

"That's a floating hotel," said Jason Goulet as he put his arm around Monica.

"It's a floating city," said Tim. "I think it has more restaurants and shops than Bath. It seemed to take us a while to reach the ship. Security had to scan each passenger card as we boarded. Security had been tight, much like an airport. We stepped onto the open promenade deck, had our cards scanned and were directed inside to the ship's atrium. People were standing around in awe as they looked upward to the eight story central atrium of the ship. Four glass paneled elevators were making their way to the different decks. The first impression I had was one of glitz. Lots of mirrors and glass with colorful lighting. There were ship's staff everywhere to direct us to our cabins. We all agreed to meet up at the Windjammer Bar right after the lifeboat drill.

Tim and I went to deck twelve in the middle of the ship and found our cabin. I opened the door to find a cabin done in understated earth tones. There was a small sitting area by the glass doors, the two beds had been pushed together to make one large one. Out on the balcony were two comfortable chairs, but it was going to have to be a lot warmer before I'd spend any time out there. The bathroom was small, but efficiently organized. It even had a bath tub, but I could tell by looking at it that neither Tim nor I would fit in it.

"Once we unpack," said Tim as he hugged me, "there's nothing else we have to do for two weeks."

"Except to show up for dinner."

"That's true. Every meal we'll have to decide what to eat."

"Sucks to be us," I laughed.

**

It was three o'clock in the afternoon when the signal for the life boat drill sounded. We had been warned by numerous announcements over the loud speakers telling us when and where to report. We all flocked to our designated stations on the promenade deck. Bundled up against the cold we all held our lifejackets in our hands as we watched the crew members explain how to put the jackets on. I wasn't sure the lifejackets would do much good in the frigid Atlantic where survival time was about six minutes.

By the time we got back to our cabin the luggage had arrived and Tim and I unpacked our bags. There was more than enough storage in the small cabin for our things, and by the time we finished unpacking it was time to head up to the bar and meet with the others.

Monica and Jason were already at the bar when we arrived. We took a table and Ronda and Jackson joined us shortly after. The waiter came over, took our order and brought us our drinks.

"I saw Billy working his ass off down at the excursion desk. There was a line forming as people wanted to book their shore activities. He said he would join us for dinner after the excursion desk was closed," said Rhonda.

"Have any of you looked at the excursions yet?" I asked.

"No," said Tim. "Let's get Billy's recommendations first."

"Great idea," replied Jackson.

"Anybody see Parker?" I asked.

"I'm sure he's going to be very busy until after sail away."

"Speaking of sail away," I said. "We should get ready to go up on deck with the others and watch the Boston skyline recede into the distance."

"We should be sailing out at five. We'll be able to see the sunset over the Boston skyline," Tim said looking at his watch. "Just enough time to finish our drinks, grab our jackets and head up on deck."

It was cold up on deck, and we brave souls bundled up as we watched the Boston skyline recede in the distance. The sunset over the harbor was a brilliant red with streaks of cold blue clouds. The cold wind was in contrast to the brightly lit up ship, and we all hurried inside to escape the dark and the cold. I found it hard to believe that in two days we would be running around in shorts and commenting on the warm weather.

Our gang was assigned the eight o'clock seating in the dining room. The dress code on the first night was informal. We went to the Blue Ocean Bar for drinks before heading into the dining room to find our table. Billy Simpson, dressed in his white uniform, was already at the table when we arrived.

We were greeted by our waiter and assistant waiter, who passed out the menus and took our orders.

"Billy," I said when the waiter left to place our orders. "You look great." Billy was not only fit and trim, but he gave off an air of confidence that I had never seen before.

"I wasn't sure I'd make it to the end of the day," he said. "Turn around day is the toughest day of the cruise."

"Turn around day?" asked Monica.

"It's when we come into port. We disembark passengers and welcome aboard the new travelers, plus all the luggage of the departing passengers has to be taken off and new luggage brought aboard. All crew members have to have something to do."

"You have to move luggage?" asked Jackson.

"No, I have to direct lost passengers and do a room check to make sure everyone is off the ship."

"But the rest of the voyage you work at the excursion desk right?" asked Rhonda.

"Yes, and I can tell you it's busy all the time."

"But do you like it?" asked Jason.

"I freaking love it," said my friend Billy.

"Where's Parker?" I asked.

"Helping sail the ship. He'll have dinner with us tomorrow, which is the first formal night by the way."

"Do you get to see him much?" asked Rhonda.

"Only at night. They let us bunk together," said Billy.

"That's an enlightened attitude," said Jackson.

"Remember this is a European cruise line. They are much more advanced than prudish North Americans."

"So" I began, "What do you recommend for our excursions?"

"Leave it up to me," said Billy smiling with pride. "I'll take care of it and send the tickets up to your cabins."

Did I mention that I was proud of Billy?

Chapter 9

We were headed into warmer weather. I woke up sometime around sunrise. Tim was still sleeping so I went out on the balcony for some air. It was still chilly, but much warmer than the weather in Boston had been. Cruise ships move very slowly so I calculated that we were off the coast of Virginia this morning. By tomorrow we'll have crossed over the Gulf Stream and be in warm weather for sure.

I threw on my sweats and flip flops and headed up to the buffet to get some coffee, hoping that no one would see me. No such luck, as I filled my coffee cup at the coffee urn I turned around and there was Monica and Jason. They waved me over to their table where they were having breakfast.

"Nice outfit," said Jason.

"Blow me," I responded.

"Someone got out of the wrong side of the bed," added Monica.

"What does that even mean?" I asked.

"No idea," replied Jason. "How did you sleep?"

"Sea air and travel. I slept soundly."

"Where's Tim?" asked Monica looking around.

"Still sleeping, I think."

"Speak of the devil," said Jason as Tim walked into the buffet and spotted us.

"I figured you'd be here," he said to me.

"I'm sure the note I left on my pillow helped."

"It was a clue. I'm a detective, remember?"

"Hard to forget," remarked Monica as she rolled her eyes.

"Has anyone seen Rhonda and Jackson?" I asked.

"I don't think they're morning people, and it's what time now?"

"A quarter past seven," I said looking at my watch.

"What should we do today?" Tim asked.

"I think we should get some breakfast, clean up, and walk around the promenade deck a few times. Then explore the ship," I offered.

"Let's check the bulletin board and see what else is happening today," said Monica.

"Sounds like a plan," said Tim. "But now I'm starving. Let's eat."

I took three trips around the buffet just to make sure that I didn't miss anything. I filled up my plate. By the time I got back to the table Rhonda and Jackson had appeared and pulled up two more chairs.

"Decide to join us?" I asked.

"Chill out Ashworth," said Rhonda. "It's vacation. Actually it's hard to sleep past six now."

"I know," agreed Tim. "When you're young you can't wait to retire so you can sleep in the morning. The cruel irony is that by then you are so conditioned to getting up early and you no longer need as much sleep."

"So what's good here?" asked Rhonda as she looked at our plates piled high with breakfast food. "Never mind, I think I'll find out on my own."

**

Back in the cabin I shaved, showered and dressed for the day. It was still cold so I bundled up in layers for outside walking. Half an hour later I found the rest of the group, minus Billy and Parker since they were working.

"When does the excursion desk open?" I asked.

"The hours are eight to noon, and two to four," said Tim who was smart enough to bring the ship's newsletter along with its lists of activities.

"I think we need to walk off breakfast after we stop and talk to Billy," offered Jackson.

There was already a line at the excursion desk, even though we had another two full days at sea before we arrived on the first island. There were three clerks at the desk and when it came our time to be waited on, Billy took over."

"I'll wait on these clowns," he said to his coworkers. They looked shocked.

"Clowns?" I asked. "I hate clowns."

"I wanted to shock those two goody goodies I work with," he whispered. "They are way beyond serious."

"What do you have lined up for us?" asked Tim.

"I've already booked the group on several tours, and I think you'll like it. Horseback riding on the beach, jet skiing in the bay, jeep tour into the jungle, that sort of thing. Parker and I will go with you on one or two of these if we can get the time off."

"They give you time off?" I asked.

"Just a few hours here and there. Anyway your tickets will be delivered to your cabin with the time and meeting place on them.

"What should we do now?" I asked Tim as I looked at my watch.

"How about a game of mini golf?"

"Let's go."

We had a foursome for golf. Monica and Jason joined Tim and me on the top sports deck. It was windy and the glass walls that enclosed the golf course did little to mitigate the breeze. We each grabbed a score card and pencil and made our way through the course. At the end we compared scores and suffice it to say I didn't have the top score.

"How about a swim?" suggested Tim.

"I'm up for it," answered Jason.

"It's going to have to be a lot warmer for me to get in the water," I said. Though truth be told the air temperature was now hovering in the seventies. Still it wasn't warm enough for me to do the swimming thing.

"I'm with Jesse," added Monica. "I'm going for coffee."

"I'm going with Monica," I said. "Have a good swim."

"Let's head out to the coffee bar," I said. "I could use a good latte."

"We can check out the bulletin board while we're there."

I still had a hard time figuring out where everything on the ship was located. We walked into the sports deck elevator and took it down to the Centrum lobby area. The glass elevator gave us a view of the eight-story central lobby, and we realized that the coffee shop was one deck above the lobby. We got off and took the grand staircase up to the next deck. We ordered our drinks and then headed over to the bulletin board and read the notices.

"Friends of Bill W," read Monica. "That's an AA meeting isn't it?"

"Yes, it is."

"What's this 'Friends of Dorothy' and who's Dorothy?"

"It's Dorothy from the Wizard of Oz. You know 'Over the Rainbow.'"

"I don't get it."

"It's code," I said. "It's the gay and lesbian meeting."

"Okay, I get it now. But look at this one." She was pointing to a notice tacked up on the board. I read it:

Spirit Circle

Navigator Room Deck 10

3:00 pm

All Welcome.

"Shit!" was all I could say.

Chapter 10

Monica and I took our coffee out to the pool and watched Jason and Tim swim. They were the most striking-looking men there. Tim has a hard body with six pack abs that's rare for anyone his age, and Jason at six foot seven makes everyone around him look like a midget. Like most of the longer cruises the average age of the passengers was heavily in the elderly category. Looking around I wasn't feeling too bad about my age, being a decade or so younger than a lot of my fellow passengers.

They got out of the water when they saw us. "I just called Rhonda and she and Jackson are going to meet us for lunch in the Copenhagen Dining Room at noon," I said.

"Okay," said Tim. "I need to go back to the cabin and change."

While we were out the steward had cleaned the room, changed the towels, and made up the bed, and brought us a fresh bucket of ice. On the freshly made bed was an envelope addressed to both of us. I opened it while Tim slipped out of his wet swim trunks and began drying himself off with a towel.

"It's an invitation to dine at the captain's table at eight-thirty."

"How did that happen?" asked Tim. "That's quite an honor."

"I'm sure Parker Reed had something to do with it."

"Yes, that's got to be it," Tim agreed.

"You might want to put on some clothes," I said. "You're distracting me."

"That's kind of the idea, Jesse."

**

It was lunch time and the Copenhagen Room was the smaller of the two main dining rooms and was glitzy with cut glass chandeliers and lots of gold framed mirrors. It had floor to ceiling windows that looked out on the stern of the ship. The six of us were taken to a table by the windows where we had a great view of the ocean and the wake of the ship as we slipped through the Atlantic. The efficient wait staff filled our water glasses, passed us menus and brought a basket of bread.

"I could get used to this," sighed Rhonda. Today she was dressed in a 1970s pant suit. Where she got her clothes I could never figure out. Some of them, I suspected, she had saved from previous decades.

"We'll have to do this again," said Jackson. His silver hair was brushed back and he was wearing tan slacks, sandals, and a green polo shirt. I was so used to seeing him dressed up in a shirt and tie that I had a hard time adjusting to the new look.

"Jason and I will probably sign up for another cruise before we get off this one," added Monica. She was wearing a blue sleeveless dress and Jason was in shorts, white sneakers with white socks and a brightly colored print shirt. He was dressed just like the more elderly gentlemen on the cruise. I refused to wear old man white sneakers, preferring my L.L. Bean sandals.

"Did anyone else get an invitation to dine with the captain tonight?" I asked. They all nodded their heads. "I'm sure Parker is behind the invitation."

"It's quite an honor," agreed Rhonda. "I can't wait."

"Okay, I know you too well," said Rhonda to me. "Something is bothering you. Out with it."

"There's a spirit circle that's meeting at three this afternoon," I said. They all looked at me like I was crazy.

"So?" asked Jason. I looked at Monica and she took up the narrative.

"You know our family were Spiritualists." They all nodded. "Spiritualism isn't just about talking to the dead. It's also a religion. Our grandparents were real Spiritualist. Our great grandfather was one of the founding members of modern Spiritualism. Spiritualism lost its credibility because there were and are so many fakes and charlatans. Jesse and I have doubts about Spiritualism and don't practice it, or really believe in it, but we feel that we have a duty to our family to defend true believers and save them from exploitation."

"You mean," interrupted Tim, "that you feel duty bound to expose the charlatans."

I reached over to grab his hand. I knew he understood.

"Exactly," answered Monica. "Those who prey on peoples' grief and despair for money are the worst human beings out there."

"So," Jackson said as the first course of lunch arrived, "you're going to the meeting to debunk the frauds."

"We're going," I answered, "with an open mind. If we see fraud, we will debunk it."

**

At three o'clock Monica and I took the glass elevator up to the Navigator Room on deck ten. When we arrived the room had around twenty-five people milling around. This was a typical presentation room with a podium at the front and stackable chairs placed in neat rows. Monica and I took seats in the back. A woman whom I guessed to be in her thirties seemed to be in charge. She was dressed conservatively in a gray business suit and had an abundance of silver jewelry. She stepped up to the podium.

"Welcome to the Spirit Circle here on The Prince of Denmark. My name is Nancy Gilliam and I'll be the facilitator. This is my assistant Jerry Callahan." Callahan was tall and dark and somewhere in his forties.

"The best way to describe a spirit circle is as a group gathering with the purpose of spiritual growth. In our seating we seek to contact loved ones who have passed from this earthly existence into the next," said Callahan as he stood up next to her.

Nancy Gilliam continued, "I am a minister in the Westminster Spiritualist Church in Boston. We are a religious body in the Christian tradition who seek to develop our spiritual gifts and break through the bonds of our physical limitations. Spiritualism is a religion that believes that the spirits of the dead have both the ability and the desire to communicate with the living.

"Spiritualism began as a movement in the nineteenth century that sought to contact those who had passed from this life. Our religious roots can be traced back to Emanuel Swedenborg in the eighteenth century. Swedenborg claimed to be able to talk to the dead and gave descriptions of the spirit world.

"In 1848 the Fox sisters claimed that they were able to communicate with the dead using rapping sounds. Later in life they admitted that this was a hoax, but then later still they recanted their admission. The time after the American Civil War was the time of greatest growth in spiritualism. In their grief those who had lost loved ones in the war sought comfort by contacting their loved ones through mediums. Unfortunately this was also a time of greatest fraud and deception as less scrupulous practitioners began to perpetrate fraud for the grief-stricken. Elaborate theatrical performances of mediums became the norm with the use of spirit trumpets, spirit boxes, ghostly materialisms, ectoplasm, table tilting, Ouija boards and so on. These were often revealed to be nothing but parlor tricks, thus aiding the decline of spiritualism.

"World War I was a time of resurgence for the Spiritualists as the grief stricken once more sought to contact their loved ones. One of the foremost advocates of the Twentieth Century was none other than the author of Sherlock Holmes, Sir Arthur Conan Doyle. Conan-

Doyle sought to prove the validity of mediumship through a more scientific means as he traveled about and studied various mediums and looked for fraud.

Modern Spiritualism began in the late Nineteenth Century by Sebastian Ashworth and then in the mid nineteen twenties by his son, Wilson Ashworth, and Harry Stackpole. These two men founded what would become the first institute to establish an academic foundation for the study of parapsychology. Ashworth himself was a powerful medium and Stackpole was an acknowledged as a great psychic. Both men were responsible for the growth of interest in the paranormal."

Monica and I looked at each other as Nancy Gilliam talked about our great-grandfather Wilson Ashworth. We had to acknowledge that her presentation was a fair summary of the movement, but we were still unsure of her motives.

"Today's meeting is for information only. I plan on facilitating a sitting tomorrow if there is interest. An ideal circle would be ten to twelve people. How many would be interested?"

Almost everyone in the room raised their hand. Quickly looking around I could see this was a group of various ages. I wondered if the recent surge of interest could be traced to the television mediums that have become popular on cable stations.

"That's a good number. If you are interested I'll be here tomorrow at three on our last sea day before we reach Aruba. There are some rules that I'd like you to keep in mind. Please be prepared to gather at least ten minutes before the circle. Please do not wear heavy perfume and please avoid alcohol. Please leave your cell phones in your cabin. Let go of any expectations you have and come with an open mind. And now let's end with a brief prayer to Spirit."

At the end people got up and quickly left the conference room. I figured they must all be late to bingo or something. Monica and I headed out when Nancy Gilliam stopped us.

"For some reason," she said looking at us and waving us back into the room, "Spirit thinks I should talk to you both."

"Any idea why?" asked Monica, though I was pretty sure we both knew why.

"I'm seeing a family Bible," she said. "That's the image that Spirit gives me when there is a strong tie to family of the past. I sense you too are closely related and not husband and wife."

"I'm Jesse Ashworth and this is my cousin Monica Ashworth Goulet."

"Ashworth?" she repeated. The color had drained from her face.

"Sebastian Ashworth was our great-great grandfather and Wilson Ashworth was our great-grandfather," said Monica.

"I wondered why Spirit was so strong in the room. You both have the gift; I can feel it."

"I think we better sit down and clear the air," I said. The three of us took chairs and moved them into a small circle. "Our grandparents were practicing Spiritualists but our parents rejected spiritualism. All that we learned was from our grandmother. Though we are open minded, neither of us practice Spiritualism. In fact we are probably skeptics. We are here to make sure that there is no fraud. We don't want to see people hurt."

"This is good news," said Nancy somewhat to our surprise. "I agree with you that there has been too much fakery and fraud and this has made our movement suffer. I welcome your skepticism and feel you will be a great addition to the circle."

What the hell was going on?

Chapter 11

We had promised to meet the gang at four o'clock for a drink at the Seafarer Bar. The bar was decorated like a Maine seafood shack. Lobster buoys on the wall and fish nets hanging from the ceiling. When Monica and I arrived Tim, Jason, Rhonda, and Jackson were already there. Billy and Parker were, I guessed, working somewhere on the ship.

"How was the séance?" asked Rhonda. She was wearing a bright red Hawaiian muumuu. Really? Jackson had on a Hawaiian shirt of the same fabric.

"Aloha," I said. "It wasn't a séance; it was more of an informational meeting. The spirit circle will be tomorrow." I had to bite my tongue and look away from them. Not to be critical, but we were far from the South Pacific.

"Do you think it's fake?" asked Tim.

"She gave a good background of the movement," answered Monica. "But then anyone can search the web for information. We're going with an open mind, but we will be looking to see if she is just giving a cold reading."

"What's a cold reading?" asked Rhonda.

"A cold reading is when the so-called medium makes some general statements to the room and waits for a response," I explained. "Then with some leading questions and the reading of body language the fake medium is able to convince the grief stricken that they've received a message from beyond.

"For instance I might walk into a room, look around and say 'someone here has lost a parent.' It's a pretty safe bet with a room full of the middle-aged. 'I feel a male presence stepping forward.' Then I look about the room for a reaction. I spot my mark and then walk over to her. 'I feel this message is for you, so know that your father is stepping forward. 'Did he have a pet name for you?' At this point the mark is hooked in and will answer the questions. You see how it works?"

"It looks easy," said Rhonda. They all nodded.

"Some of them are highly skilled," added Monica. Then she mentioned the name of a prominent TV medium. "Years of practice have made him proficient in cold readings. Just watch him closely on TV sometime."

"Why do people fall for this?" asked Jackson.

"People want to believe in something and those fakes take advantage of that," I answered.

"The bastards," exclaimed Rhonda.

"Exactly," I agreed.

**

It was the first formal night of the cruise. If you wanted to eat in the main dining rooms, you had to dress up. Those who chose not to dress could find other venues for dinner. Tim and I had brought along sports jackets and ties, and we were dressed and ready to go. Since we were dining at the captain's table tonight we didn't want to be late. Tim came over and checked my collar and looked for lint on my jacket. Not finding any he hugged me.

"Sometimes I forget how lucky I am," he said.

"I couldn't imagine this life five years ago. Moving back home after thirty years, I thought I'd retire and just fade away. I never imagined I'd have a whole new life. When you pulled up in front of my home in your police cruiser five years ago you changed my life."

"That's how I felt. When I saw that you had moved back my heart began to beat a little faster. I was convinced I'd never see you again when you went off to college."

"Keep it up and we'll never make it to dinner."

"I guess we better get going," he said reluctantly.

Once we reached the public areas of the ship we could see that everyone was dressed up. It reminded me of a high school prom night, except that everyone was hideously old. It was like a Halloween horror movie played in slow motion. The ships photographers were everywhere snapping photos and taking formal portraits of couples against a backdrop of the ship at night. One of my favorite things to do is go to the photo gallery and look at the photos. The camera is not everyone's friend.

Tim and I showed the head waiter our invitations and he led us to the captain's table. Parker Reed was already at the table. He was dressed in a white uniform that showed up his blue eyes and curly black hair.

"Your old boyfriend looks pretty hot in that uniform," Tim whispered to me as Parker stood up to greet us.

"You should see him out of uniform," I whispered back.

"Welcome," said Parker as he gave each of us a hug. I noticed my hug was just a little longer than Tim's. Just then Billy appeared and he, too, was dressed up in a uniform. Crew members all wear uniforms and each one has a badge with an insignia that indicates what their position on the ship happens to be. I wasn't all that familiar with the insignias, and had no idea what those insignias meant.

The head waiter was coming our way with the rest of our group. At six foot-seven it's always easy to spot Jason in a crowd. He was dressed in a brown sports coat followed by Monica in a long red dress with a black shawl. I couldn't see Rhonda at first because she was behind Jackson, who was dressed in a black tuxedo. I was relieved to see she was dressed in a simple blue gown, but it appeared to be from the 1960s. Still it could have been much worse. I remember one New Year's party when she dressed as Jackie Kennedy in the blood stained pink suit.

The waiter came over and poured glasses of wine from one of the two bottles on the table. Very discretely he poured club soda into Billy's glass. Off in the distance I could hear the tinkle of glass and silverware and above it all was the sound of a piano playing Brahms. There was a sudden flurry as the captain arrived. We all stood as he came to the table. The captain was probably somewhere in his fifties and had more gold braid on his uniform than anyone else on the ship.

"Captain Jorgenson," said Parker, "Let me introduce my friends. This is Jesse Ashworth and Tim Mallory, Rhonda Shepard and Jackson Bennett, Monica and Jason Goulet." We all shook hands.

"Pleased to meet you all. Parker has told me much about you." The captain had a slight Scandinavian accent. "I understand that you two run a detective agency," he said to Tim and me.

"It's our retirement project," I said.

"And you two," he said to Rhonda and Jackson, "run a gift shop and an insurance agency. And the two of you are retired and occasionally work for the detective agency," he said to Monica and Jason. "Please sit."

We sat down and the captain offered a toast to good dinner companions.

"Thank you for inviting us," I said to the captain. "It's quite an honor."

"It's a pleasure to meet the friends of my two newest crew members." Both Billy and Parker were beaming. The waiter gave us menus. Lobster was the special of the evening.

"Is this Maine lobster?" asked Rhonda.

"With a ship sailing out of New England we wouldn't dare serve anything else," said the waiter.

The captain kept the conversation going through dinner and showed a genuine interest in us, which I guess is what makes a captain a captain. We were just about to dig into dessert when the head waiter rushed over and whispered into the captain's ear. The captain stood up immediately.

"Please excuse me. There is something I have to attend to," he said and hurried out of the dining room.

"That's not good," said Parker as he got up and hurried after the captain. We all looked at Billy for an explanation.

"No idea," he said. "I work for the cruise and activities division. The captain and his crew are in charge of sailing the ship. I'll find out later when Parker comes back to the cabin."

"Is it my imagination," said Monica, "or is the ship turning?" There did appear to be movement of the ship. It was subtle but we were definitely turning

A few moments later there was a call on the ship's PA system. "Oscar! Oscar! Oscar!" The dining room waiters all looked at each other and some rushed out of the dining room. Billy shot out of his seat. We all looked at him.

"What is it?" I asked.

"Man overboard," said Billy as he rushed out of the room. Just then we heard three blasts of the ships whistle.

Chapter 12

The quick turn of the ship was disorienting and once we had made a complete turn, the ship slowed to a stop. Passengers were ordered to stay off the promenade deck. Tim and I went to our cabin and stepped out on the balcony where we had a view of the attempted rescue. Flares were sent off into the sky and shortly we were in the company of other boats. We watched as the crew lowered a small lifeboat that we knew was also the rescue boat. It was small and fast and had a large searchlight on it.

We must have been in a shipping lane because it didn't take long for the other ships to show up. There were two large oil tankers and an even larger freighter, along with a smaller sailing yacht. Off in the distance I could see lights on the shore.

"Where are we?" I asked Tim.

"We're somewhere off the coast of Venezuela. Those are the lights over there. We're near Aruba. Venezuela is rich in oil which is why there are tankers nearby. We watched as the other ships launched their own rescue boats. The captain came on the PA system and on the cabin speakers to update us on what was happening.

Before long we saw several navy vessels arrive. It was difficult to tell what country they were from, but it looked like they were taking over the rescue mission. Around midnight we heard the ships engines start up and the ship slowly began to move along.

"Nothing we can do," I said as we watched the navy boats disappear in the distance. "Time to get some sleep."

**

Parker had left us a message that he would meet us for breakfast in the main dining room at eight thirty. When we arrived we were surprised to see him seated with the captain.

"Good morning," said the captain as he and Parker stood while we were seated. "Please sit." The waiter came over and poured us coffee. If you want good service, it pays to dine with the captain. We were given menus, and we gave our orders as the waiter headed off to the kitchen.

"Parker tells me you've had some success with missing person investigations. I'd like you to look into this man overboard case. The authorities are going to have some tough questions, and I'd like to have some answers. I've been authorized to offer compensation for your time."

Tim looked at me before he spoke. I nodded. "You have your own security team here. We don't want to step on any toes."

"You'll have full cooperation with security. In fact I think they might be relieved to have some experienced help. None of them has had a man overboard case on any of the cruises."

"What type of compensation?" I asked.

"We'll pick up the tab for this cruise, plus any expenses. In addition we'll give you a voucher for a future cruise at our expense."

"Fair enough," said Tim. Just then the waiter hurried over with our breakfast, and I tucked into my plate of eggs benedict.

"After breakfast," said the captain, "I'll go over the information that we have gathered so far. I just have a feeling that it's not going to end well."

**

The sea was calm and had the brilliant blue that only the Caribbean seems to have. It was warm and every deck chair was taken up by northerners who were determined to get their share of the February sun. Tim and I grabbed coffee to take back to the cabin. The cabin was made up when we returned from breakfast. Luis, the cabin steward, seemed to have the ability to be invisible. Whenever we stepped out of the cabin, we returned to a freshened and made up room.

Taking our coffee we sat out on the balcony and looked out on the endless sea. "I didn't intend for this to be a working vacation," said Tim.

"I rather like a good mystery, but I fear that this is more tragedy than mystery. But our expenses will be paid and we get a free trip, so that's a win." Looking at Tim as he relaxed in the chair I was struck yet again on how handsome he is. Not just for his age, but for any age. He had the jaw and cheekbones that would be the envy of any movie star. Unlike most men well passed fifty he had rock hard abs and a flat stomach. While I had to exercise to keep in shape, Tim seemed to naturally be formed like a Greek Apollo.

"What are you thinking about?" asked Tim waving his hand at me. I must have been day dreaming.

"I was thinking that you look like a sixty-year-old Greek Apollo."

"Is that a good thing?"

"Oh, yes, that's a very good thing."

"You're not half ugly yourself," he replied with a wink.

"Anyway," I said getting back to the job, "I fear that if the navy hasn't found the missing man by now, there is no chance that he is still alive."

"We need to go meet with the captain and get all the facts."

"But for the next ten minutes, let's just sit here and gaze out at the endless ocean."

**

The captain met us out on deck and took us down into the working section of the ship. No wood paneling or carpeting here. This was basic work and living space for the crew. We were led into the rather large security office. Two officers were monitoring a bank of security camera screens. We were issued crew badges, which I guess made it official that we were working for the cruise lines.

Captain Jorgenson introduced us to Pierre Hudon, the head of security. He greeted us with a slight French accent.

"Pleased to meet you both," he said as we shook hands. He was about five-nine and appeared to be in his thirties. The dark tan attested to the fact that he spent some of his time outside.

"I'm very proud of my international crew," said the captain. "Officer Hudon is from Belgian."

"How can we help you Mr. Hudon?" I asked.

"This has the potential of being a publicity nightmare. It would give our investigation credibility to have two outside consultants on the case."

"Give us the facts," said Tim. "Let's see what we can come up with."

"The missing man is Jeffery Donovan, age thirty-six. His wife reported him missing when he didn't return to their cabin."

"What time was that?" I asked.

"She reported him missing at eight-thirty last night."

"And that's when you notified the captain?" asked Tim.

"Yes."

"I think," I said, "we need to interview the wife and look at the cabin. Did you pick up anything on the security cameras?"

"Yes, just after dark we have a shot of him walking along the promenade deck." He took us over to the security monitors and had one of his officers show us the video. He emerged from the ship onto the deck and walked toward the bow. He disappeared into the shadows. "Once he's at the bow of the ship we lose sight of him."

"He jumped for the bow?" asked Tim.

"We don't know. The bow cam doesn't show us anything. The ship's bridge is above the bow, and we keep the bow dark so we have visibility on the bridge at night."

"It appears," I said, "that he was carrying a backpack. Did you find a back pack on the bow?"

"No, we didn't find anything."

"People are always out on the promenade deck. Did anyone see anything?" asked Tim.

"Looking at the security tapes, there appeared to be about a fifteen minute window when no one was walking to or from the bow."

"So he most likely jumped from the bow of the ship where there was no camera visibility and took his backpack with him," I was finding it a strange thing to do. "If it was suicide why take the backpack? There's nothing in there he would need."

"People are bat-shit crazy," said Tim shaking his head. "We would like to review all the tape footage from around the time he went missing."

Hudon led us over to one of the security camera consoles, pulled up two chairs and gave us basic directions on viewing the tapes.

Chapter 13

The sun was bright and Rhonda and I found two chairs in the shade on the promenade deck. Rhonda and I have known each other for over thirty years. We both taught English at Amoskeag High School in Manchester, New Hampshire, and when Rhonda retired she bought a gift shop in my home town of Bath, Maine. I followed her there and life has never been the same. This was the first time we'd been alone since we set sail two days ago.

"You're doing what?" she exclaimed. "I can't believe you're working on your vacation."

"I don't think it's going to be much of an investigation. It looks like suicide. I think the cruise line just wants to look like it covered all the bases."

"And you're looking into the spirit circle nonsense for fraud, don't forget that."

"It may not be nonsense," I said defensively. The fact was I thought it most likely was fakery.

"You and Tim need some time to be together."

"We work together every day and we live together, so I don't think there's room for more time. Besides look who's talking. You and Jackson haven't even set a date. Tick tock!"

"Well," sighed Rhonda, "you know my track record with marriage." It was true. Rhonda had been married several times, along with other long and short term relationships. Still I had seen a remarkable change in Rhonda since she had moved to Bath.

"Let go of the past. You know very well that we aren't the same people we were five years ago."

"I know," she nodded. "Looking back at all the years at Amoskeag High, they all seem to blend together. It's almost like I was sleep walking all those years. Now life is full and each day is a new adventure. I love my life."

"I feel the same way," I admitted. "You know I loved teaching, but that was all about giving and making a living. Now it's about living and joy."

"What did you do with Tim by the way?"

"He's out exploring the ship and most likely checking out the bow of the ship to see how easy it would be to jump overboard. And Jackson?"

"He went to the casino to some type of slot contest. So what are you doing for the rest of the day?

"Let's see," I said looking at my watch, "we're all meeting for lunch in about half an hour, then Tim and I are going to talk to the wife of the jumper and check out the cabin, then Monica and I are going to the spirit circle and check it out with a critical eye. I'll probably take a short nap before we all meet for drinks and dinner, then we're off to the show."

"I'm going to the scrapbooking workshop this afternoon and Jackson and I will catch the show later," she said getting up. "See you at lunch."

**

Jeffrey Donovan's cabin was one deck above my cabin on the starboard side of the ship. We took out the key card we had been given and let ourselves in.

Donovan's wife, Julie Donovan, had been given another cabin because this cabin could be a potential crime scene.

"How can this be a crime scene," I asked Tim, "if we know that he jumped from another part of the ship?"

"We don't know why he jumped," answered Tim, "and we don't know if it was suicide or not. There may be clues here that could help us. Remember we only deal in facts. All we know for a fact is that he most likely jumped overboard. But someone could have hidden up there and pushed him off. Security cameras have been tampered with before. So let's look around."

The bathroom was empty except for the towels that hadn't been changed. The closet had no clothes, and I assumed that Julie Donovan had packed up her stuff. The three life jackets were still on the top shelf as were the rolled up beach towels. The bed remained unmade, and I figured the cabin steward was instructed not to touch anything. I knelt down and looked under the bed. I saw a black object and reached for it. "Look what I found," I said.

"A cell phone? Excellent," said Tim.

Tim checked the built-in drawers and we both went out on the balcony. I looked over the railing. "Why jump from the bow of the ship?" I asked. "Why not from the cabin balcony?"

"Look down that way," said Tim pointing to a black object about six cabins down.

"A security camera?" But if it was dark it wouldn't make any difference would it?"

"Probably not," Tim agreed. "But the bow is closer to the water. It's a long drop from up here."

"But if your goal is to kill yourself, what difference would it make?"

"Good point," said Tim. "Let's drop the phone off at the security office and see if they can find anything on it."

"Where to now?" I asked.

"Let's interview the wife and see what she has to say."

**

It was evident that Julie Donovan had been crying. Her eyes were red and swollen and her hair was a mess. We introduced ourselves, and she led us into the small sitting area of her cabin.

"Are you here to help the cruise line cover this up?" she asked defensively.

"I can assure you," said Tim. "that if we find that the cruise line is in any way at fault, we'll be the first to blow the whistle."

"As full disclosure," I added, "the cruise line is covering our expenses, but we are independent contractors with no loyalty to anyone but the truth." Julie seemed to relax.

"Can you tell us the events leading up to your husband's disappearance?" Tim asked.

"We spent the morning at the pool and then we went our separate ways. I went off to the spa, and he went off to play a round of gulf. We were supposed to meet back at the cabin before lunch, but he never showed. It wasn't like him not to show up. By eight o'clock I contacted security. They were certain he was somewhere on the ship, so they began looking for him. When they checked the security video they saw him head to the front of the ship, but they never saw him return." Here she began sobbing, and we figured we got as much information as we were going to get.

"I'm sorry for your troubles," I said as I handed her our business card. I had scribble our cabin number on it and circled my cell phone number.

"What do you think?" asked Tim as we left her cabin and headed down the long passage way.

"Something about this whole thing doesn't ring true," I said. "I can't put my finger on it, but something is missing."

"Is that opinion or intuition?" he asked. Tim knew there was a difference.

"I think it's a little bit of both. What do you think?"

"I think there are some missing pieces here that we need to find. I think we'll have to interview the wife again. It just seems to me that she should be asking us some questions. If two security agents came to your door what would be the first thing out of your mouth?"

I thought about it for a minute or two. "I'd ask if there was any news. She seemed to assume that there wouldn't be."

"Of course it might not mean anything. People grieve and handle stress differently, but we should keep it in mind."

"Next step?"

"Call Derek and have him run a check on Black Broker for Julie and Jeff Donovan. We paid for international cell service, so we might as well use it."

I took out my cell phone and hit speed dial. The call didn't go through. Then I realized I had to use the country code first. It took a while, but finally the call went through.

"Bigg-Boyce Security Agency, this is Jessica. How may I help you?"

"Good to hear your voice," I said.

"Jesse, is everything alright?"

"Everything is fine. We're having a great time. How is everything there?"

"Not much happening here. Derek upgraded an alarm system for the coffee shop and that's about it. And before you ask, Jay and Argus and Jake are having a blast at Eagle's Nest. He had us over for dinner last night. He's almost as good a cook as you are."

"The reason I called is because we need you to do a search on Black Broker."

"You two aren't working are you?"

"Sort of," I said. I told her about the missing man who was believed to have jumped off the ship. She said Derek would be in later today, and they both would do a little research. She would call back when she had more information."

"We love you guys," she said and then disconnected. There was one more place I needed to stop. I took the glass elevator down to the main deck lobby. There was a line at the excursion desk. People were making last minute plans for Aruba. I stood in line. There were two women working the desk. I didn't see Billy anywhere. When my turn came I showed them my security badge and asked for Billy. The young woman stepped out into a back room and returned with him.

"Hi, Jesse. What's new?" I held up my badge and told him that Tim and I were looking into the disappearance of Jeff Donovan.

"How can I help?" he asked looking somewhat bemused.

"Can you tell me if he and his wife have booked any excursions for the trip?"

"Yes, I can look it up on the system. But what does that have to do with someone jumping overboard?"

"Probably nothing, but on the other hand people don't usually plan for the future if they are planning to kill themselves." While I was talking Billy pressed some keys on his console and looked at the screen.

"What's their cabin number?"

"They're in cabin 1125."

Billy hit a few more keys. "No they have nothing booked."

"Interesting, Thanks Billy."

"See you at dinner tonight."

"Will Parker be joining us?" I asked.

"I'm not sure. The captain has been keeping him busy."

"I guess that's a good thing.

"I guess it is," sighed Billy.

Chapter 14

The afternoon atmosphere was brilliant with fresh, warm sea air and bright sunshine. I hated the thought of being inside even for an hour or so as I stopped at Jason and Monica's cabin. There cabin was similar to ours, but they had a window rather than a balcony, and they were on a lower deck.

"Where's Jason?" I asked as I entered the cabin.

"He and Tim are off by the pool catching some sun as he put it. We could skip the spirit circle and join them."

"We could," I agreed, "but this is about more than just checking out some spirit circle. This is about facing up to our past."

"I know. I can feel it, too. We need to be there, though I'm not sure exactly why."

"We were brought up with mixed messages. Our grandparents taught us Spiritualism. Our parents rejected it, though they never said why. In fact I always had the impression that they feared it. But we both know that we are intuitives and like it or not it's part of our heritage."

"I just don't know if I'm ready to face up to it."

"Ready or not, they opportunity is here. Let's see where the journey takes us."

**

The Navigator Room was set up with chairs in a circle and Nancy Gilliam was at the door greeting everyone as we all entered. Jerry Callahan was seated in the back of the room. There were about twenty people gathered which meant that this would be a group reading rather than a real séance. I felt real energy in the air and as I looked over to Monica I could see that she felt it too.

"This seems very familiar," I whispered to her.

"I feel like I'm back at Gram's spirit meeting."

"Let's start with a short meditation," said Nancy as she stood in the center of the circle.

> "Oh great Spirit of Love and Harmony
> who watches over the universe and this
> beautiful earth, our home, open our
> hearts that we may hear Your voice
> among the din and noise of our everyday
> lives. Show us Your way and incline us
> to listen to the voice of Spirit that resides
> in all of us. Bless us and protect us as we
> gather here today. Blessed be."

Nancy, I was glad to see, had resisted the urge to dress for the part and was dressed in shorts and a flowered blouse. I'd seen too many fake mediums dressed up in flowing robes and silver jewelry, thinking that their theatrical accoutrements would add validity to their performance. It didn't.

"Did someone here lose a brother," she said as she looked around, "because I have a brother energy that's stepping forward." We all looked around the room and an older woman timidly raised her hand.

"Did he die in an accident? Because Spirit is showing me that he had a quick passing." The woman nodded her head but didn't speak. "Did you bring something of his to the meeting today?" Again the woman nodded.

"I brought his picture with me," she said as she reached into her purse and brought it out.

"Know then that this is his way of acknowledging that he knows what you are doing, and he thanks you for your prayers."

Nancy was beginning to look tired, and she sat down in an empty chair. She looked around the room. "Spirit is showing me an eagle sitting on a nest. It's not one of my usual images so I don't know what it means. Does anyone understand the image?" I raised my hand, as I thought of my home Eagles Nest.

"An older woman is stepping forward. She's showing me a cane with a silver handle. It looks like the handle is shaped like an angel. I think this image goes to you," she said looking at Monica. The color drained out of Monica's face and she nodded. "She thanks you for taking such good care of it."

Nancy herself was looking very pale, and she ended the session with a brief meditation. Some of the people seemed disappointed that they didn't get a message. Others seemed to be just curious.

Several people stayed behind to talk to Nancy as Monica and I headed out to the promenade deck. The sea was calm and smooth as glass, though it didn't seem like we were moving very fast. Parker had said that sometimes the cruise ships just circle around out on the ocean because the islands are so near. I knew we weren't that far from Aruba.

"What do you think?" I asked as we slowly walked along the deck.

"It was a limited reading. For all we know the woman who got the reading was a friend of hers and it was a set up. As you know sometimes a fake medium will seed the crowds."

"And my reading isn't anything that she couldn't find on line. I wrote two cookbooks, so if she googles my name I'm sure Eagle's Nest will come up since I refer to it in my writer's bio."

"What about me and Grammy's cane?"

"I didn't know you even had it," I confessed. "I'm not sure how she got that information."

"Verdict?"

"More evidence needed," I said. "We can't rule out the theory that this was nothing but a cold reading, or that she had done some basic research. After all she knows who we are and if she is a true follower of Spiritualism, then she knows all about our family as well. There are literally hundreds of pictures of our grandmother with her cane. We are the only grandchildren so it wouldn't be a stretch to guess that one of us had it."

"Your father or my father might have been given it."

"Not really. Both of our parents rejected Spiritualism, and we were trainees, so it's logical that one of us would have been given it."

"I guess you're right," Monica sighed.

"You really would like to believe that Nancy Gilliam is the real thing, wouldn't you?"

"I guess I really would like to believe that there is something after death." Both of Monica's parents had died last year. My parents, though still alive and living in Florida, seemed to me to be getting frail."

"Why do you think our fathers turned against Grammy and Grandpa? What made them reject Spiritualism?"

"I don't know. All I know was that we were all at Lilydale when something happened and our parents took us home." Lilydale is a Spiritualist community in Chautauqua County in New York state that is the center of the modern Spiritualist movement. Each year about 22,000 visitors go to Lilydale for workshops, church services, group medium demonstrations and private readings. It is part church community and part occult amusement park without rides or midway. As a child Monica and I, with our parents, went to stay for part of the summer with our grandparents who had a summer cottage there.

"I never asked my father about it. He let me go with our grandparents, but they never went back again."

"I asked," said Monica, "but I never got a good answer. All I ever heard was mumbling about fakery or something. Too late to ask them now, I guess."

"Unless," I said carefully, "we use the medium to contact them."

"A private reading? That might be a good test of our Miss Gilliam."

"Let's see if she can come up with information that she couldn't possibly know about."

"Yes, and if she doesn't, she's toast."

Chapter 15

Billy didn't make it to dinner; the excursion desk was open late to accommodate the passengers who decided to take an excursion at the last minute. Billy had sent out tickets to our cabins late that afternoon. He wanted it to be a surprise. We would be going horseback riding along the beach in Aruba, and honestly I couldn't think of a better thing to do.

Parker was once again waiting for us at the table and once again he was dressed in his white uniform. While I don't have a clothing fetish I have to admit that uniforms and suits and ties are a turn on and Parker looked exceptionally good in his. This was a casual night so Parker was the only one dressed up at the table. Rhonda was wearing a 1950 sun dress with a matching scarf. "Is that from the Donna Reed collection?" I asked her.

"That's funny coming from a Tommy Bahama model."

"This is from L.L. Bean, you witch," I said indicating my shirt.

"No bickering at the table," said Parker. "Unless you want some time in the brig."

"You have a brig on board?" asked Jackson.

"Oh, yes, and we get to use it on occasion, too."

"I'm going to guess it's usually alcohol related incidences," said Monica.

"Speaking of alcohol," said Rhonda. "Where are our drinks?"

"Here they come now," answered Jason as he took his from the waiter's hands.

"To us," said Parker as a toast.

"To us," we all responded. I suddenly felt a hand in my lap and since I could see both of Tim's hands on the table I deduced it didn't belong to him. Parker, however, sitting on my left seemed to only have one hand visible. I was saved further embarrassment when the waiter passed out the menus and parker had to grab it with his right hand.

"Funny guy," I whispered to him behind my menu.

"Just checking for old time's sake.'"

"Not going to happen," I said and then added just to be a tease, "tonight."

Everyone was looking at me. I must have missed a question. "I'm sorry. What did I miss?"

"Jackson just asked you about the spirit circle," said Rhonda.

"Do you think it was real?" Jackson repeated.

"Real is a subjective term," I said trying to hedge a little. "If you believe that spirits exist and that they want to talk to you, then it may possibly be real. On the other hand, if you believe that the physical world we live in is the only reality, then of course the whole thing is fake."

"Okay you two," said Tim with exasperation, "I've about had it with your maybe, maybe not attitudes. I've watched the two of you for the last five years. You've both proved time and again that your instincts and intuition are right on target. And you've both been extremely vague on your family background, and I think it's time we all heard the truth."

Monica and I looked at each other, and I was about to speak when the waiter came over with the bread bowls and took our orders. I was saved for the moment. As soon as the waiter left with our orders, everyone looked at me. Monica took up the narrative.

"Our great grandparents Wilson and Olivia Ashworth, along with Harry Stackpole, were founding members of modern spiritualism. From 1914 to 1933 they ran a spiritualist summer camp up in Adams Township, Maine. Both of them were said to be gifted mediums, having shown what we would call psychic abilities from the time they were teenagers. They had two children, Joseph and Sadie. Joseph inherited the gift of channeling the dead. Sadie did not, but she later married a medium from Lilydale.

"Joseph married our grandmother Alice, who was herself a medium, but by the 1940s spiritualism was on the decline. Both were high school teachers who spent their summers at Lilydale. Their children were Clyde and Joe Junior. Clyde is Jesse's father and Joe Junior was mine. Neither son seemed to have any ability at all, and I think that situation somehow estranged them from the rest of the family. Intuitiveness or whatever you want to call it often skips a generation. At a young age Jesse and I both began having 'experiences.' Our parents had no problem at first with our grandparents training us.

"But something happened at Lilydale in the late sixties that turned them against spiritualism altogether. By then though we were old enough to defy our parents and continue our training, but once we both went off to college we began to have second thoughts about the whole thing. Science and psychology seemed to be a better explanation for the world around us than ghosts and spirits. In short, we no longer believed in anything other than this physical realm. But then Jesse moved back to Bath, and I left my ex-husband Jerry Twist and moved back to Bath, too. Once we were together again, we seemed to gain back our intuition. Jesse, by the way, is a gifted medium."

Suddenly everyone at the table was looking at me like I was caught with my hand in the Salvation Army bucket. "I guess trying to debunk the spirit circle has dredged up a lot of old baggage. The whole spiritualist stuff scares the crap out of me for your information."

"So this Nancy Gilliam," asked Parker, "is she real or fake?"

"It's hard to tell," I answered, "but I'm leaning toward fake." I looked at Monica, and she nodded her head. "She did say some things that hit home, but nothing that couldn't be researched if she knew where to look. Though I think she really believes she has a gift."

"Well," said Parker, "we can't have fraud on the cruise. If you find out that she is charging money for anything, you need to report it to security."

"If I find out," said Monica with grim determination, "that she is exploiting people's grief, she's going to need security."

"Sorry for the delay," said the waiter as he appeared with our dinners, "there was an incident in the kitchen."

"What type of incident?" asked Parker.

"One of the big carving knives is missing. Chef is having a fit."

**

After dinner I stepped out onto the deck to get some air. Reliving the family history had left me feeling drained. I prefer the bright physical world of everyday reality. I didn't really believe in spirits; I didn't disbelieve either for that matter, so it always sends me off balance when I'm reminded of it. My attitude about life after death was simple: it either exists or it doesn't, so whether I believe it or not is immaterial. Still there was one reality I couldn't ignore. Whenever the little voice in my head tells me something, I better listen. It was telling me something now, but I couldn't quite make sense of it.

**

Tim and I were sitting on our cabin balcony having coffee and watching the beautiful Caribbean morning as our ship was pulling into the port of Oranjestad, Aruba. It would be good to be on solid ground again, but I had to admit that I really love sailing. The pilot boat was leading the ship to the docking facility, and we could see the fuel barge waiting for us. Our excursion wasn't until afternoon so we were at leisure until then.

"Can't we just sell everything and live on cruise ships?" I asked. "No cleaning, no cooking, no worries."

"No family and no Argus," he reminded me.

"Never mind then. But I could do this a few times a year."

"That we could do."

Suddenly there was a loud knocking on our door and a muffled voice coming from the corridor. I got up to answer it. Tim followed close behind. It was Parker Reed, and I could tell by his face that something was wrong.

"We've had an incident," he said.

"An Incident?" asked Tim. Parker looked around the corridor and motioned us back into the cabin and closed the door behind him.

"You were investigating that medium Nancy Gilliam weren't you?"

"Yes, Monica and I have been watching her."

The cabin steward went into her cabin to clean this morning. Nancy Gilliam was stabbed."

"Stabbed?" I asked stupidly.

"She's dead."

It looked like Monica and I wouldn't be getting a private reading after all.

Chapter 16

Tim, Rhonda, Monica, Jackson, Jason, and I walked off the ship a little after noon and were greeted by our tour director whose name was Erik. Billy was out there with the other excursion staff directing passengers to their assigned tours. Parker, I'm sure, was busy on the ship.

The captain had decided not to notify the authorities in Aruba about the murder of Nancy Gilliam. In all likelihood she was murdered in international waters and to get the Aruban authorities involved would most likely delay the cruise. I agreed. Nancy Gilliam would still be dead regardless of who investigated the murder. Whoever did it was on board at the time, and so we already had a list of suspects. The fact that the list included about four thousand people, however, was going to be a headache.

Erik herded our little group to a small air conditioned van. There were two other vans of passengers who would be going horseback riding, and it looked like there would be about twenty of us altogether.

Aruba was a surprise. I was expecting a lush tropical island with lots of palm trees and humidity. Aruba was dry and desert like with cacti everywhere. The air was dry and warm, and I had a hard time reconciling this paradise with the fact that it was the middle of February. Erik took us on an island tour before we ended up for our horseback riding tour. We stopped at the California lighthouse which had fantastic views of the ocean and then on to see a group of huge rock formations that had ancient pictographs carved in them. Wherever we stopped I took out my camera and snapped pictures.

We arrived at the stables where we were served light refreshments while the horses were being readied. Most of the group had never ridden before. Only Monica and I had experience on a horse. As teenagers we rode often. My mother's brother owned a farm in Dresden, and he had a stable of horses. It had been forty years since I'd been on a horse, and I hoped it was like riding a bicycle.

Once we were all saddled up Monica and I found ourselves at the end of the herd. The less experienced riders were up front with the guides, with one guide bringing up the rear. We headed down a narrow path to the beach, and we proceeded in single file as we went. I couldn't get a good look at the rider in front of me, but there was something vaguely familiar about him, but then sometimes I have an overactive imagination.

Once we reached the beach we were able to spread out. Our horses were raring to go on the hard-packed beach.

"Nice day for a ride," said the rider in front of me as he pulled up beside me.

"The weather is perfect, and I understand that there's a winter storm bearing down on New England. I think it makes it all that much sweeter to be here."

"You don't remember me, do you?" I looked at him. and he did look familiar, and then it hit me. "Mr. Dexter?" I barely recognized my old high school music teacher.

"Hello, Jesse. Bill Simpson said you'd be on this cruise. I bet he arranged for us to be on this excursion.

"He told me you were the entertainment director on this ship." Monica cleared her throat. "I'm sorry; this is my cousin Monica Goulet."

"Pleased to meet you," said John Dexter.

"And you as well," she replied. "What type of student was he?"

"Very talented voice back then. Have you done anything with music, Jesse?"

"I sing in the church choir, but that's about it."

"This is my wife Margery," he said as a smallish, younger looking woman rode up beside him. "We met on a cruise a couple of years ago. I lost my first wife to cancer, and then lost all my investments, but when I met Margery everything changed." Margery beamed at him. We did our introductions and then caught up with the rest of the group.

The guide had us pick up the pace, and he rode the horses down to the edge of the water. Tim was up front of the group with the inexperienced riders along with Rhonda, Jason, and Jackson. When we caught up with them, I could tell that they loved the experience.

"Being on horseback felt so natural, and then I remembered that until recently, this was how humans traveled.

"I love this," exclaimed Tim as I rode beside him. "Let's plan to do this again."

"I'd love to. Did you see the guy I was talking to back there?" I waved to Jason to join us.

"No, why?"

"That's Mr. Dexter, our old music teacher." The three of us maneuvered our horses over to where he and his wife were riding. Jason and Tim greeted them.

"Please call me Brent," he said. "I'm not your teacher anymore. And I'm only a few years older than you guys." Brent seemed to know all about us because Billy had filled him in on all his old students. "Be sure to catch the shows. I'm directing several musicals on this cruise."

"We will," I promised.

All too soon the ride was over, and we were back in the parking lot getting ready to board the white vans back to the ship. Brent Dexter slipped me a note when no one was looking. I read the note and it said "please see me. I'm in cabin 6120." Yes, this could be interesting.

**

"We had to move the body," said Pierre Hudon the head of security, "but I took plenty of photos." Tim and I were sitting in the security office as he showed us the photos of the crime scene. The images certainly were bloody. "I know the U.S. authorities are going to want us to collect as much evidence as possible. I've already contacted the coast guard, and they'll be meeting us in Columbia."

"Why Columbia?" I asked.

"The United States has a military presence off the coast because of all the drug traffic. That will give us a few more days to investigate. I can't tell you what a public relations nightmare this is going to be."

"I can imagine," replied Tim. "But if we can help resolve this soon, we may be able to mitigate the damage, after all this is not the fault of the cruise line."

"The cruise line would be very grateful and generous I'm sure."

"So she was stabbed to death?" Tim asked, though the photos made it quite clear.

"Yes, she was," Hudon was looking sick to his stomach.

"Was it the knife that went missing in the kitchen?" I asked.

"What knife?" I filled him in on the gossip we heard from the waiter. "I think we need to visit the chef."

Hudon led us down to the main dining room and into the kitchen. I had never been in a cruise ship kitchen before. It seemed to be several smaller stainless steel kitchens all connected together and seemed to go on forever. We found the head chef who was supervising other chefs. The whole place was a beehive of activity. Hudon signaled to the head chef and excused himself and came over to us.

"I understand that a knife went missing at dinner last night," Hudon said.

"Knife went missing? I did not hear that. Hey," he yelled over to the other chef, "Did a knife go missing?"

"Yes," said one of them. "I could not find it, and I had used it earlier."

"What did it look like?" asked Tim. Looking around there seemed to be lots of knives, and they were all different sizes.

"It looks like this one, except that it had a red handle." the chef said as he picked up a large ten inch knife. It was in fact exactly like the knife in Nancy Gilliam's back.

"Was there anyone in the kitchen yesterday who did not belong here?" Tim asked the group of chefs.

"We gave a kitchen tour to a group of passengers yesterday," offered the head chef.

"Then we need to see who organized the tour and who was on it," I said.

"Yes," agreed Hudon.

**

I got a text message from Derek saying that he had some interesting information on Jeff Donovan that Black Broker had uncovered. Unfortunately I'd have to wait until the next port to find a wireless connection because of all the data that Black Broker produced. Data on the ship was too slow and too costly. We would arrive tomorrow in Willemstad, Curacao and I'd look for a wifi connection.

"There is way too much stuff happening on this cruise," I said.

"It's a working vacation," said Tim. "I think we'll need a vacation from our vacation after this."

Chapter 17

We docked in Willemstad in the early morning. I had a feeling that the ship had cruised the night slowly since Curacao wasn't all that far from Aruba. Last night we could see the distant lights of Venezuela from our cabins balcony, and I had to admit that despite the investigations we had taken on, it was a restful time, and if nothing else we had escaped the cold grip of winter.

Tim and I met Rhonda, Jackson, Monica, and Jason in the Copenhagen dining room for breakfast. Billy had signed us up for a tour of the city as an orientation. He suggested that we would enjoy exploring the town on our own after the tour.

"What's new?" asked Rhonda once we had settled down at the table and ordered breakfast.

"Well," said Tim, "we've got a man lost overboard and a psychic medium murdered, and we've been asked to help out security, and I think that for a vacation that's more than enough excitement."

"You guys seem to attract cases wherever you go," added Jackson as he sipped his coffee.

"It does seem that way," I said. "I don't mind doing one case at a time, but it seems like one case leads into another."

"It's no coincidence," said Monica. "We were meant to be on this cruise." We all looked at her. "It's a feeling I have. Ask Jesse."

"I have to agree," I said as they all looked at me. "I feel we were meant to be in this particular cruise, but I don't know why."

Our food arrived, and we were quiet for a few minutes while we dug into our breakfast.

"So," said Rhonda, "I don't understand who would want to kill a medium, or why."

"All we know for sure was that she was stabbed with a knife with a red handle and that the knife probably came from the kitchen," I said. "We have no motive. As for opportunity, she had an inside cabin so the only way the killer could get into the cabin is if they had a key card or she let them in."

"There were no signs of a struggle that we could see," added Tim. "So it's likely she let the killer in."

"So it's possible that she knew her killer?" asked Jason.

"Yes," I replied, "it's possible."

"So what are you two going to do today?" asked Rhonda.

"We're going on the tour with you," I answered. "Then we're going for a drink in a nice waterfront bar with wifi."

**

Willemstad is a scenic town with colorful Dutch style buildings lined up along the waterfront. We left the ship and were taken over by van to the town, though it really was near enough to walk if we had to. We boarded a train-style tram with open cars and had a pleasant tour of the town. The most unique feature of the town is the Queen Emma Bridge, a floating pontoon bridge that connects the Punda side of the town with the Otrobanda side of the town. The bridge swings open at regular intervals to allow marine traffic to pass by. When the bridge is open there are ferries to transport people from one side to the other.

On the Punda side of the town is the floating market, a picturesque and unique market place made up of floating fishing boats from Venezuela. After the tour Tim and I opted to get off in town while the others headed back to the ship.

We walked over the Queen Emma Bridge and just got across when the bridge signal sounded. We watched people scurry off the bridge and then watched as the bridge swung aside to let a fishing vessel pass.

"Nothing like this at home," I said.

"Only when the Carlton Bridge used to open up." The Carlton Bridge is the iconic vertical lift bridge that connects Bath and Woolwich. It's been replaced by a newer bridge that was built beside it. The new bridge has better traffic control, but lacks the charm of the old one.

"Now it's swinging back. Whoever thought to build a bridge on pontoons?"

"Someone who didn't have to worry about ice flows."

Tim and I wandered around like the tourists we were and finally found an outside bar with wifi. We ordered beer, and I took the laptop out of my backpack and powered it up. Derek had sent me three files on Jeff

Donovan from Black Broker. I angled the laptop so Tim could read along with me. As we read through the documents Tim let out a low whistle.

"I'm thinking Jeff Donovan didn't commit suicide," I said as I looked at the documents.

"Suspicious death if nothing else," said Tim.

"No body was found and no evidence that he survived."

"I think we need to question the wife again." There were two very interesting facts that had come to light. Jeff Donovan owed a lot of money to a lot of people. He was an investment broker and was being investigated for fraud. It also appears that he had just taken out a very large insurance policy.

"I'll email Derek to check out the policy with the insurance company, but I'm willing to bet that the wife is the beneficiary," said Tim. "We probably better do a background check on her as well."

"I knew something was off about this case," I said. "I think we really need to look closely."

"I agree. Let's head back to the ship. It'll be a nice walk."

On the way back we met Monica and Jason who had been shopping in the little shops that line the path back to the terminal.

"You've got that look," said Monica as we looked in a gift shop window.

"What look," I asked.

"You're on to something. Is it the Gilliam murder?"

"No, I don't have a clue about that one. I think we need a closer look at the victim, and I'm pretty sure the man overboard wasn't suicide or an accident." I explained what I felt about the case.

"I think you might be on to something, and I trust your intuition."

"Thinking and proving are two very different things."

"I have no doubt that we'll solve this case before we finish our cruise. After all, crime is usually simple enough to solve once we have the clues."

"And once all the clues fit."

"This really is a lovely island," said Tim slipping into vacation mode. "I'd like to come back here sometime."

"Me, too," I agreed as I sipped my beer.

**

Back on the ship I texted Monica to meet me in the coffee shop while Tim went off to play basketball with Jason. Coordination type sports is not my thing. Give me a jogging path and I'm okay, but anything else that requires timing and grace and I'm out.

"I haven't seen Rhonda and Jackson since we got off the tram ride," said Monica as she watched the barista make our lattes.

"Me neither. I don't think they're good at relaxing. They both work hard, and it seems like they've been keeping busy doing as many ship activities as they can squeeze in."

"A deck chair in the shade and a good book, and I'm good until dinner."

"I was hoping for that, but as you know trouble likes to find me."

"Trouble, as you call it, is what you were meant to do."

"I guess," I said as I grabbed my latte, and we headed for a table.

"Anything on the Gilliam murder?" she asked.

"I don't think so. I need to check with security later and see where they are. They're trying to keep the murder under wraps."

"Can they do that? Shouldn't they contact the authorities?"

"The murder happened in international waters, so it's a gray area. They will have to answer to US authorities once we land in Boston, but I think they'd like to solve it before then."

"Do you think anyone else is in danger?"

"No, I think she was targeted."

"That's the feeling I have, too. Do you think it was because she was a medium?"

"I think there might be more to it than that" I said. "One thing is for sure."

"What's that?"

"The killer is still aboard."

Chapter 18

Pierre Hudon was busy taking notes as Tim and I sat with him in the security office.

"How did you get this information?" he asked obviously impressed.

"We have our sources," answered Tim.

"It still could be suicide," said Hudon. "If he owed a great deal of money and was looking at a long time in prison, he may well have decided to kill himself. You said he took out a large insurance policy before this trip?"

"Yes," I agreed. "He did. But we don't know anything about it yet. We have our office looking into it."

"It could also be murder," added Tim. "He lost a lot of money for a lot of people. Someone onboard could have hidden in the bow and pushed him overboard."

"You think that's what happened?" asked Hudon.

"No," answered Tim. "But it is a possibility that we have to keep in mind."

"Now," I said switching the conversation, "what can you tell us about Nancy Gilliam's death?"

"The chef positively identified the knife as the one that went missing. Nancy Gilliam was traveling alone in cabin 3162, which is an inside cabin. The steward found the body. The shop's doctor said she died of a knife wound to the chest. There appears to be no evidence of a break in, so she must have let the murderer into the cabin."

"This much we already know," I said to Hudon. "What can you tell me about her?"

He passed us a file which Tim picked up to read aloud. "Nancy Gilliam age thirty-six. 2038 Brockton Street, Boston, Massachusetts. No emergency contact information."

"All we have is the passenger information that she filled out. We retrieved her passport from the cabin, but it doesn't have any additional information."

"May I use your phone to call our office?" I asked. "We can check for any additional information."

"Sure, go ahead."

I called the agency and Jessica answered. I told her that we wanted any information on Nancy Gilliam that she could get.

"If we can find a good wifi connection in Cartagena tomorrow," I said to Hudon, "we should have some good information. No offense, but the Wi-Fi on the ship sucks."

"Yes, it does, but it's the best we can do until someone comes up with a faster satellite connection. Not to mention that we have lots of passengers using the internet which slows it down."

It was time for Tim and me to meet the others for a drink as the ship prepared to depart from Willemstad. I love sail away; it's fun to watch the activity on the dock as the cables are loosed and brought aboard and as the ship slips slowly away from the dock with the pilot ship escort.

We found a table on the top deck's Sunshine Bar. Monica and Jason were already there when Tim and I arrived. Rhonda and Jackson were late. When they appeared Rhonda was wearing a red silk kimono with her hair done up in a bun with chop sticks stuck through it. The only thing missing was white face paint.

"I didn't realize tonight was costume night," I said as they sat down. Jackson was dressed in normal shorts and polo shirt.

"Very funny," she said. "Tonight is formal night and this is my frock. I wanted to try it out first."

"Your very own geisha," I said to Jackson. "You're a lucky guy." Jackson winked at me. Just then I saw Billy Simpson come up the stairs.

"Billy!" exclaimed Jason. "They let you out?" Billy pulled up a chair and joined us.

"I'm on break for a little while. I'll be joining you for dinner. Parker, too."

"Great," said Monica. "Let's all get our pictures taken together."

"That shouldn't be hard to do," replied Billy. "Those photographers are all over the place on formal nights."

"Where are you sending us tomorrow?" I asked Billy. "This will be the first time I've set foot in South America."

"I've arranged for a walking tour of the old city followed by a carriage ride."

"Oh, that sounds like fun!" said Rhonda clapping her hands."

"Isn't Columbia a dangerous place?" asked Monica.

"Not for tourists," replied Billy. "They're trying to build up the tourist trade."

"Another round?" asked the waiter as he passed by with a drinks tray. We all looked at each other.

"Line 'em up!" said Rhonda pointing at our empty glasses.

**

I looked in the mirror and sighed. I couldn't seem to get my hair just right. I like to have my hair free flowing because I'm grateful to have hair at my age, even if it's streaked with silver. I picked up a bottle of hair gel. Squeezed some on the palm of my hand and ran it through my hair. I tied my tie and ran my hand over my white shirt to straighten out the wrinkles.

"Looking good," said Tim coming up behind me at the mirror.

"All I see in the mirror is an old man," I said.

"You're too critical," said Tim slipping his arms around me. "You are one good looking dude no matter what your age is."

"Thanks," I said.

"And if we had time, I'd show you."

I turned around and hugged him. "You're the best guy in the world."

**

The dining room was festive. The chairs had been covered with white coverings that matched the tablecloths, and flowers in glass bowls appeared on each table. Even the servers were liveried in white uniforms. As promised the photographers were out, and they had set up Caribbean backdrops in the public areas for formal photos. All eight of us posed for a group picture. Billy promised that he could get us a deal on the pictures if we wanted them.

Tonight's choices included prime rib, Caribbean jerk chicken, tilapia, and vegetable pie.

I placed my order: shrimp cocktail, Caesar salad, prime rib, and flourless chocolate cake. Everyone at the table ordered prime rib. Parker offered a toast, and we raised our glasses.

Suddenly the lights went out and there was general confusion. Quickly the lights came back on and Parker got up from the table and hurried out of the dining room.

"I think formal nights are cursed," said Rhonda as she sipped her drink.

"I better go see what's going on," said Billy as he got up from the table and hurried out.

"What just happened?" I asked the waiter as he came to check on us.

"I'm not sure," he said. "Security is looking into it now."

Suddenly there was a scream from a nearby table. "My necklace is gone," screamed a woman sitting by a window. I looked around the room and saw other women checking themselves for their jewels.

All the nearby servers rushed over to the table and started looking on the floor for the missing necklace.

"Just an educated guess," said Tim as he sipped his glass of wine, "but I'll bet that power outage was just a diversion for the theft of the necklace."

"Great," I said. "So we have a jumper, a murder, and a jewel theft on this cruise."

"And lots of good food," said Rhonda as the appetizers arrived.

Chapter 19

Pierre Hudon, the head of security, looked at us as we sat in his office. "This is going to be a publicity nightmare if we don't do something before we return to Boston.

"The theft of the necklace was a professional job," said Tim adopting his police persona. "I'm guessing it wasn't costume jewelry."

"It was worth about twenty thousand dollars. It was made up of emeralds and diamonds."

"Someone had to know where the light switch was," observed Tim.

"You might want to ask the dining room staff if anyone was asking them questions about the lights," I offered.

"Yes, good idea," Hudon replied. "Anything new on the Donovan case?"

"We should have some information when we check in with our office tomorrow," said Tim. "What about the cell phone we found?"

"It was a burner phone, but we know a call was placed to Aruba."

"What about the kitchen tour?" asked Tim. "Do you have a list of who was on it?"

"No, we don't. It was open to anyone."

"Well, keep us up to date," I said.

Tim and I got up and headed out on deck. "Inside job?" I asked.

"That's what I was thinking, but I didn't want to say that to Hudon."

"He didn't ask our help on this one."

"No, but I bet he would accept any help he could get."

"We have two other cases to tackle first," I reminded him.

"True."

"Though I have a feeling that we'll solve one very soon," I said.

"A feeling? God help us."

I looked at my watch. "We have just enough time to catch the evening show. It's going to be a musical review, I think."

"Let's go, then," said Tim as we hurried to the theater.

**

The white modern structures of Cartagena appeared on the horizon as we were eating breakfast in the dining room. Billy had explained that there were two parts of the city: a modern section with tall skyscrapers, known as the *Bocagrande*, and an old walled city.

"What time is our carriage ride?" asked Monica.

"The tour meets at ten on the dock, and then we'll be taken to the old city," I replied.

We glided into the port and passed by the statue of the Virgin Mary in the center of the inner harbor. Once we were docked we headed off the ship and gathered at the end of the pier. Billy and the other excursion workers were busy organizing the different tour groups, as we stepped onto the van that would take us off for the day. The van drove along the narrow, winding streets of Cartagena's dock yards and into the city. Just outside of the walls of the older city the van stopped, and we were given twenty minutes to shop in the little boutiques that were ensconced within the ancient walls.

**

I'm not a shopper, so Tim and I found a bench under a shady tree, and I pulled out my laptop from my backpack. Luckily I was able to tie into a public wifi signal and search my email. Derek had been busy, and he had sent some of the insurance documents as an attachment. I quickly downloaded the files as the van driver started to round us up.

"We'll have to look at these when we're back on the ship," I said as I powered down the device.

Our next stop was the inquisition museum where various articles of torture were on display. The Spanish Inquisition held trials of those accused of crimes against religion. According to Billy, almost every tour of the city included this museum on its route. Rather than listen to the details of extreme torture I wandered out to the garden and snapped some photos of nearby buildings.

"Couldn't stand being in there could you?" asked Monica as she came up behind me.

"Extremely bad vibrations in there," I answered.

"I know; I felt it, too."

"Considering that I can't even go into antique shops, this place was a real challenge. Let's wait for them outside," I suggested.

In a few minutes Tim, Jason, Rhonda and Jackson came out of the museum with the other visitors.

"That was gruesome," said Rhonda making a face.

"It sure was," added Jason.

"What happened to you two?" asked Tim.

"Bad vibes," I said. They all looked at us but didn't say a word.

We walked to the next stop, the *Iglesia de San Pedro Claver*, or in English the Church of St. Peter Claver, the first saint in the new world. It was built between 1580 and 1654. We were given recorded tour devices and wandered around the huge church. While most churches exude a calm and spiritual air, there was some strange energy in this one I couldn't put my finger on, until I got to the high alter. Under the alter and behind a glass wall was the mummified body of San Pedro, which accounted for the feelings I was getting.

Our next stop was a small city square with lots of shady trees and a statue of Simone Bolivier where a group of carriages and several teams of horses were waiting for us. All six of us were able to fit in the carriage, and we started the slow clip-clop of the carriage ride. The old city was ancient and beautiful with colorful buildings that had balconies off the second floor with lots of trailing, flowering vines. It looked like a movie set of an idyllic South American city.

The hour long carriage ride came to an end and the van took us back to the ship. We each went separate ways. I looked at my watch and headed to the theater where rehearsal for the show Breaking Dawn was being held. Brent Dexter had invited me to the rehearsal. Brent saw me and waved me over where he gave me a music folder.

"Look this over and don't breathe a word of it," he said in a conspiring whisper.

**

Two days later we hadn't achieved much progress on the case. "You're being very mysterious," said Tim when I returned to the cabin. Tim was stretched out on the bed with a book. "Disappearing for an hour or two every day."

"You know me," I said hoping to cover, "I like to have an air of mystery."

"So I just read some of the documents that Jessica emailed us again, and she just sent two new ones. You want to take a guess as to who benefits from Donovan's death?"

"The wife, of course," I replied.

"Interestingly, no."

"No?"

"Well, yes she gets the money from a life insurance policy and it is quite substantial."

"So she does benefit? I don't understand."

"The bulk of his money, the money he made bilking investors, goes to the Westminster Spiritual Church."

"What?"

"He leaves everything in his will to the Westminster Spiritualist Church."

"And that," I said, "changes everything."

The theater was almost full when we arrived after dinner. Parker and Billy were down in the front row and had saved seats for us.

"Why the front row?" asked Rhonda. "There are better seats in the back."

"I like to be close to the action," I said. "I've heard this show is really good. I ran into Mr. Dexter today and he said not to miss this."

"It's a musical revue," said Jackson. "But I don't know what the theme is."

"I've heard," I said, "that it's music from the Second World War. It's called Breaking Dawn."

"I love that music," said Rhonda.

"Reminds you of your early twenties, does it?" I asked.

"Don't be an asshole," she replied.

"I need to run to the men's room," I announced to the group.

"The show's about to start," warned Tim.

"If I'm late I'll sit in the back until I can sneak back between numbers," I answered and headed out of the theater.

Backstage was a beehive of activity. I waved at Brent Dexter and he gave me the high sign. He said I could watch the opening numbers from the theater wings. The first act was a song and dance number by three singers made up to look like the Andrew Sisters.

The next act was a band number by a Glenn Miller tribute band. The chorus line dancers dressed in their 1940s costumes danced the Jitterbug to the music of the band. From the wings I could see my friends in the front row as the stage lights spilled onto the first row seats. They were totally caught up in the show.

By attending all the rehearsals I knew very well what the next two numbers were going to be. The first was a lone singer on a dark stage dressed in an Army Air Corps uniform singing Johnny Mercer's "Sky Lark." Then the singer would be joined by men and women in uniform singing "On a Wing and a Prayer," with a backdrop of moving airplane propellers.

I checked the buttons on my uniform, straightened my tie and walked out on a dark stage and stepped up to the microphone. The spotlights came on, and I began to sing "Sky Lark." Out of the corner of my eye I could see my seven friends looking up at the stage with open mouths. They had all heard me sing in the church choir, but I never sang solo. My former music teacher, Brent Dexter, had cooked up this idea for fun, and I wanted to surprise everyone.

When I finished the applause from the audience pierced through me like a gunshot, and I realized why people so single-mindedly sought out a career in entertainment. Lights came up on stage, and the men and women of the chorus came out in uniform as I began the first verse of "A Wing and a Prayer." They joined me for the next verse, and I had to keep up with them as they danced around the stage. When the number ended I went backstage, and Brent Dexter gave me a hug and whispered "good job" in my ear.

"Thanks for the opportunity," I whispered back. "The look on their faces was priceless." By the time I scrubbed off the makeup and changed my clothes the show had ended, and I slipped back into the theater to join my friends as they were leaving.

"You were amazing," said Monica as she hugged me.

"You are good at keeping secrets," said Tim.

"I almost died of shock," complained Rhonda.

"It was Mr. Dexter's idea," I said and Billy, Tim, and Jason, who had been students of Mr. Dexter nodded their heads knowingly.

"He always went in for shock value," said Billy.

"This was beyond shock," said Jackson. "Now if you're ready, I'm buying drinks for everyone."

Chapter 20

Pierre Hudon was busy taking notes as we filled him in on Donovan's will and the insurance policy. "That is rather a large insurance policy and a possible motive for murder," he said. "Except," said Tim, "we can't place her near the bow of the ship and security footage doesn't show her anywhere near the outside decks."

"But we do know that there was some type of connection between Donovan and Gilliam," I added. "Why else would he leave his money to the Westminster Spiritualist Church?"

"I've got the office checking out anything they can find out about the church and Nancy Gilliam," said Tim.

"The coast guard wasn't much help in Columbia. They took lots of notes, but offered little help. But we've been in contact with the FBI about Gilliam's murder. They're going to meet us in Panama," Hudon said as he shuffled some papers on his desk. "The problem is that there is a storm just off the coast, and we've been delayed, so we have another sea day before we reach Colon."

"Hopefully," said Tim, "that will buy us enough time to solve the murder."

"This voyage has been a complete disaster, sighed Hudon. "A man overboard, a woman murdered, and a jewel thief."

"I'm afraid I have one more bit of bad news," I said as I tossed a bulletin board notice on his desk. "I believe there is a fake psychic onboard who will be trying to bilk people out of money."

"Spirit circle?" asked Hudon as he read the notice. "What is that?"

"It's a group of people interested in connecting with the dead led by a spiritualist medium. The group was started by Nancy Gilliam. It seems that someone else is planning to take over the group. My cousin Monica and I attended the first two sessions."

"You don't really believe in that stuff do you?" he asked.

"We were there to see if we could identify fraud. We both have some experience in that area." I didn't explain what that experience happened to be.

"We can't have passengers cheated out of their life savings," Hudon said. "We need to stop it. I'll get my security team to shut it down."

"Whoa!" I said holding up my hand. "You need to be careful. Spiritualism is a religion and whether you believe in it or not, you can't shut down a religious service without trampling on religious freedom even if you are in international waters."

"But," he started to say as I held up my hand again.

"I'll look into it. If I find evidence of fraud, I'll let you know and you can shut it down. If I can't, then you'll need to back off."

"Fair enough, I guess," he conceded.

"By the way," I asked. "Did you learn anything more from Jeff Donovan's cell phone?"

"No, not really. He made a call to the Blue Heron, a guest house in Aruba. That was the only call on the phone since the beginning of the voyage.

"Why a guest house?"

"It has a very good restaurant attached to it. He was probably making reservations for lunch."

"That makes sense," said Tim. "But if he was making lunch reservations for himself and his wife, then he wasn't thinking suicide was he?"

"Good point," said Hudon.

Tim and I got up to go and assured Hudon we would keep him informed if we learned anything.

"I don't think you exactly made his day," said Tim once we were out of the office.

"Play your cards right," I said giving him a friendly little shove down the corridor, "and I'll make your day."

**

Luis the cabin steward was freshening up the cabin when Tim and I returned to the room. "Mr. Tim and Mr. Jesse, I'll be done in a moment."

"No hurry," I said as he was straightening up the life jackets on the top cubby that must have shifted during the voyage. Looking at them jogged something in my memory.

"How many life jackets in each cabin?" I asked.

"Most have four," replied Luis. "Some of the larger cabins have six. Suites have more."

"Do any cabins have three life jackets?"

"No. Single cabins have two, but no cabins have three." Luis took one last look around the cabin and finished up. "Have a great day," he said and exited out the door.

"What was all that about," asked Tim.

"Nothing, really. I could swear that the Donovan's cabin only had three life jackets when we went to search the cabin."

We took the stairway up one deck to the Donovan's former cabin. We slipped in, and I went immediately to the closet area and looked at the cubby above the wardrobe. There were four life jackets there.

"I guess I was wrong," I said. "I could swear there were only three."

"Well, there are four now. But it looks like the room has been cleaned. The bed has been made up and the bathroom smells like cleaning product."

I picked up the phone and called security and asked for Hudon. "Tim and I are in the Donovan cabin. It looks like it's been cleaned. Did you release it from being secured?"

"No, I didn't. It's been cleaned you say?"

"Yes."

"Let me call housekeeping. Stay there and I'll call you right back."

In a few minutes he called back. "It seems the cabin steward forgot and cleaned it by mistake on his rounds. Do you think there was anything there that we missed?"

"No, probably not," I said. Still something was bothering me. Something just wasn't right.

**

Julie Donovan met us in O'Briens Pub on deck six. Tim and I ordered a beer and Julie ordered a glass of wine.

"You have news for me, don't you?" she asked. "You wouldn't invite me here unless you have some bad news." Her hair was bound up, and she was dressed in shorts and a flowered blouse, and had red flip flops on her feet.

"We don't have any news about your husband's disappearance," answered Tim. "But we do have some questions for you."

"The coast guard asked me all types of questions in Cartagena. They were nice about it, but I had the feeling they thought I was hiding something."

"Were you?" I asked.

"Mr. Ashworth, if I knew something that would help find out what happened to my husband I would tell you."

"Can you explain why your husband left his money to the Westminster Spiritualist Church?" I asked.

"I don't have any idea why he would do that. I never heard of the place until the coast guard asked me that question. There was no money to leave in any event. My husband was being investigated for financial fraud, he was broke, and before you ask the answer is no, I had no idea about his business ventures."

"So he had no money?" asked Tim.

"We were living on my salary as a pediatric nurse."

"Who took out the insurance policy on him?" I asked.

"He did. I knew he took out a policy when we were first married, but I had no idea it was for that much. I didn't like to think about it. Does any of this make sense?"

"Yes," I said, "I think it does."

"Can you find out what really happened to my husband?"

"We'll try," said Tim.

"If you think of anything," I said, "even if you don't think it's important, let us know."

"Yes, of course," she answered. She finished her wine, and got up and excused herself. Tim and I ordered another beer. It was a vacation after all.

"Do you think she's telling the truth?" Tim asked.

"Oh, yes," I replied. "She is telling us the truth, which is about the only thing I know for sure about this case."

**

"So here's what I need you to check on," I said into the phone. Back in Bath Jessica was listening intently, and I could hear the baby crying in the background. "Is she okay?" I asked.

"She's tired," said Jessica. "It's nap time."

"I need a list of all the people Jeff Donovan cheated."

"That should be quite a list. I'm on it. I hope you're having some type of vacation."

"You have to dance to the music that's playing."

"You think one of Donovan's clients pushed him overboard?

"I think that's something we need to consider," I answered.

"Okay, say hi to my other dad. Love you both."

"Back at you," I said and hung up.

**

Ben Wong had worked for the cruise line for over ten years according to the records. He had glowing comments from his supervisors, so he was somewhat nervous as he sat down with us in the security office.

"Don't be alarmed, Mr. Wong," said Tim putting him at ease. "You've done nothing wrong. In fact according to the records you are an outstanding worker."

"I take pride in my work, sir"

"We know there was some mix up about cleaning the Donovan's cabin," I said.

"Yes, the supervisor forgot to tell me that the room was still a crime scene. When there was no note on my cleaning list, I assumed that someone released the cabin."

"When you cleaned." I asked. "Did you find anything or see anything unusual?"

"No, in fact it was quite clean. But when I looked into the closet one of the life jackets was missing."

"Did you replace it?"

"Yes, sir. There are supposed to be four life jackets in those cabins."

"When the Donovan's were in the room, did you notice anything unusual? Anything missing? Anything that was out of the ordinary?" asked Tim.

"There were a lot of glasses from the bar, so I think they liked to drink. Mrs. Donovan had a lot of clothes, and Mr. Donovan had snorkel equipment, so I think he was a sportsman. They were very nice and tipped me ahead of time."

"So they were fairly normal then?" I asked though I knew the answer.

"Yes, they were not unusual at all." Wong, looking relieved, bounded out the door.

"It seems his story isn't going to help us much," sighed Tim.

"I don't know about that," I said. "My gut feeling is that we're missing a clue there somewhere. I just don't know what it is."

Chapter 21

At five o'clock in the morning our ship pulled into Colon near the Panama Canal. Our ship was too large for the canal, so there were numerous shore excursions available for the passengers. Billy had arranged for our group to take a paddle wheel ship through the canal to the Pacific and take a bus tour back. The Panama Canal was on my bucket list, and I was looking forward to seeing it. I remember back in junior high social studies we had a unit on the building of the canal. Then it seemed like a far off exotic place, and yet here I was.

Breakfast this morning included the legendary Panama rolls, Danish like pastries with fruit filling. It wasn't raining, which was a good thing, since I was told it often rains in Panama.

Parker had some time off so he was able to join us on the excursion. A van whisked us from the dock to the waiting boat that would take us through the canals. The boat was waiting for us and it was crowded with passengers from our cruise. As we approached the first lock a guide was giving us background and history of the canal locks over the ships loud speakers. Ahead of us was a large freighter and it was impressive to see it rise above us as the locks filled. Several places along the canal we could see the work that was ongoing as a second, larger canal was being built alongside the present canal. Apparently it was supposed to be finished soon, but its completion date keeps being pushed into the future.

As our ship rose in elevation as the lock filled we could look back and see all the ships lined up behind us on the lower elevation.

"Have you ever been here before?" asked Rhonda as she stood next to Parker.

"No, none of the ships I was on ever went through the canals. Mostly we cruised along the Atlantic coast," answered Parker.

"This is amazing," said Jackson as he removed his hat and let the wind blow through his silver hair.

"Remember our plans to travel the world when we were in high school?" asked Jason.

"We had big dreams then," I agreed. "At least some of them are coming true."

"My dreams have already come true," said Tim whispering in my ear.

"You're such a romantic," I whispered back.

"Get a room you two," laughed Monica.

"We have one, thanks," replied Tim.

Once we had cleared the Gatun Locks we sailed into Gatun Lake, which when it was first created in 1913 was the largest manmade lake in the world. In the lake we were able to see more large ships waiting their turn to head either to the Atlantic or the Pacific. When our turn came we headed into the Pedro Migeul Locks and then the Miraflores Locks, under the Bridge of the Americas and then finally at the Pacific port of Belboa.

In a matter of a few hours we had traveled from the Atlantic to the Pacific. A row of large busses was waiting for us to take us back by land to the ship. Along the way the jungle seemed to hang over the road and offered us some wildlife sightings until a cloudburst obscured our view out the windows.

"This was a nice break," I said looking out the window.

"Yes, it was," Tim agreed. "But once we're back on the ship we need to get to work."

"Why is it," I asked, "that we always seem to be working two cases at once?"

"Just lucky, I guess. Maybe it's you. You attract strange cases."

"I attract strange cases? I don't think so."

"Think about it. You and Monica get involved in some spirit circle and someone gets killed."

"I don't think you can blame Monica and me for that."

"I guess not. I wish we had some clues."

"Me, too," I agreed.

"I guess that makes us clueless."

"Yes, I guess it does."

**

Maybe we weren't clueless after all. When we returned to our cabin there was a note from Ben Wong. I looked at my watch and saw that it was late afternoon and the cabin stewards were off duty until dinner time. I took my security badge and slipped into the crew only part of the ship. I really didn't know my way around and there were fewer signs than in the passenger areas. I knew they bunked on the lowest decks of the ship, and I had seen glimpses of their lounge area at the bow.

I finally found the lounge and saw Ben Wong and his friends watching a movie. When he saw me he jumped from his chair and came over.

"I just remembered something," he said. "It probably doesn't mean anything but I thought I'd tell you."

"Okay," I said and took a seat.

"I helped the Donovan's put away their suitcases when they first came aboard, so I got to see some of their possessions."

"I see," I said not really understanding where this was going.

"When we moved Mrs. Donovan to a different cabin, I helped her pack up her husband's clothing."

"And?" I prompted.

"There was something missing. I didn't realize it at the time, but I'm pretty sure it was missing."

"What was it?" I asked.

When he told me all the pieces of the puzzle fell into place. I knew what happened to Jeff Donovan. The problem was I didn't know who else was involved.

"You have no idea how helpful you've been," I said.

"I have?"

"You have indeed."

One more crew stop to see the engineer and I might be able to close on a case.

**

"Keeping a secret on a cruise ship is impossible," said Pierre Hudon. "Rumors are flying and I think we need to let people know the truth. The crew has been inundated with questions and some people are beginning to form conspiracy theories."

"Passengers were present at dinner when the necklace went missing," said Tim.

"If it went missing," I added.

"What do you mean 'if it went missing?'" asked Hudon. Tim just looked at me like I'd swallowed a fly.

"According to the dining crew no one was near the switches for the lights."

"If one of them was the thief," said Hudon, "he or she wouldn't admit it."

"Have you looked at the crew?" I asked. "They're very attentive. Not only do they notice everything at the tables they are serving, but they also keep an eye on each other so that the pace of the dining room flows smoothly. If one of them did something unusual, someone in the dining room would notice."

"There's more to this isn't there?" asked Tim.

"When I was down in the crew quarters I stopped by to see the chief engineer. There was a problem with one of the generators, and the engineers had to switch to another generator. There was a momentary blackout while the new generator came on line."

"So it wasn't planned? So who stole the necklace?"

"I think you'll find the necklace hidden somewhere in the cabin of the owner."

"You think this was a planned event?"

"No, I think the owner saw the lights go out and slipped the necklace into her purse. I think you'll find that the necklace is insured for a large amount of money. There was just an article in the New York Times about crime on cruise ships. The story was picked up by CNN and broadcast last Monday. I think that she saw the news feature and decided to collect some insurance money."

"You're sure of this?" asked Hudon.

"Yes, I am."

He looked at Tim and he nodded. Hudon sighed and picked up the phone.

**

"What the hell?" asked Tim when we left the security office. "Are you branching out on your own?"

"Not at all, but when the little voice in my head speaks..."

"Never mind," said Tim smiling. "I forgot who I was talking to."

**

"How dare you!" screamed the indignant Betty Johnson. "You can't search my cabin without a search warrant."

"Actually, Mrs. Johnson, we can. We are in international waters and the American laws don't apply here," said Pierre Hudon in an ice cold voice. "The cruise line looks down on passengers who file false claims."

"I'm telling you someone stole my necklace."

Tim was going through the drawers of the cabin while I checked out the closet. Hudon's two security officers were checking under beds going through luggage. I closed my eyes and tried to visualize where the necklace could be.

"Open your safe," I said to Mrs. Johnson.

"I will not! It's got my money and passport in there.

"You heard the man," said Tim. "Open the safe."

"I refuse."

Pierre Hudon stepped forward. "Passengers on occasion forget the code they use to lock their safes, which is why security has a universal open code. Hudon stepped forward and entered a code at the safe's keyboard. The door swung open.

"See," said Mrs. Johnson. "there's nothing in there but some money and my passport."

"It would appear," I said, "that we were mistaken."

"I told you so," responded Mrs. Johnson.

"We weren't mistaken thinking you hid the necklace. We were mistaken thinking you were an amateur." I reached into the safe and punched the backing at the rear. It gave way, and I pulled out the necklace. "The fact that the material used to create a false backing matches the safe's lining material shows a great deal of planning."

"I'm afraid Mrs. Johnson, that we are going to have to confine you to your cabin for the remainder of the voyage," said Hudon. "In the meantime this necklace is evidence, and we'll put it in the ship's safe."

"You bastards!' yelled Mrs. Johnson as we left her cabin.

"She's lucky we don't throw her in the brig," said Hudon. "Filing a false report, creating a disturbance in a public area, attempt to defraud. I think if we do some research we'll find out that she has a criminal record. I can't thank you two enough."

"You're welcome," said Tim with a wink. "All in a day's work."

Chapter 22

Puerto Lima, Costa Rica lay off in the distance as our ship slowly churned toward the port. This was the last stop of the cruise before we headed back to Boston. Rhonda and I sat at a table on the outside café on the upper deck. Rhonda was dressed in jeans embroidered with bright colors and a peasant blouse, her hair hanging loose and held away from her face with two brightly colored barrettes. She was the image of an aging hippie.

"I've hardly seen you on this trip," said Rhonda.

"You've seen me every day."

"True, but we've hardly had any time for just the two of us."

"Well we do now, and I can tell there's something on your mind."

"I want to ask you something."

"Sure, go ahead."

"I want you to be my man of honor."

"Man of honor?"

"At the wedding. I want you to stand up with me. You're my closest and oldest friend, and I want you to be in the wedding party."

"I'd be honored, but shouldn't you ask your sister?" Her sister was also my book agent for the cookbooks I wrote for fun.

"She'll be an attendant, but I want you for the top spot."

"So you've set a date?"

"Yes, the Fourth of July."

"Great! It's about time."

"Well why wait. We are not getting any younger."

"Tell me about it. My knees creak whenever I bend them."

"On your knees a lot are you?" she asked with a wicked smile.

"Maybe. So are you enjoying the cruise?" I said to change the subject.

"I am, though the food is awfully rich. I'd love to have your tuna wiggle right now."

"Tuna Wiggle? Are you crazy?" Tuna wiggle is from my first cookbook. The book was a collection of what I call white trash recipes. Easy comfort food.

"I like comfort food, though I'm fine with surf and turf, too."

"Well when we get home I'll make you tuna wiggle for lunch."

"How's the investigation going?"

I gave her a summary of the case of the missing necklace and said I had a pretty good lead on the Jeff Donovan case. "But I've no idea who killed Nancy Gilliam or why."

"You'll figure it out. You always do."

I wished I could be so sure.

As we pulled into Puerto Lima I was able to pick up a cell signal. Apparently my carrier had service in Costa Rica, but not in northern parts of Maine. Go figure. Anyway I thought it would be a good time to check in back home. I dialed the office and Jessica picked up.

"Jesse, is everything alright?"

"I was calling to ask you the same thing."

"We're fine. Jay and Argus are fine, and tell Monica and Jason that Jake is fine. No need to worry."

"Did you dig up anything on Judy Donovan?"

"Clean as a whistle as far as I can tell. No arrests, nothing shady."

"Okay, that answers one question."

"Now Jerry Callahan, on the other hand, that's a different story."

"The assistant at Westminster Spiritualist Church? What did you find out?"

"He got his start as a performer in nightclubs."

"That's not exactly a crime," I said.

"No, but get a load of this. He was a magician."

"I see."

"No you don't. He was a mentalist. His act was reading the minds of the audience. It's all trickery of course."

"And perfect for pretending to contact peoples dead relatives. Good work Jessica. Monica and I are going to give him a bad day."

"Say hi to my dad and love to you both."

"Hug that baby for me. See you in a few days."

**

The bus whisked us away from the port into the edge of the jungle where an old narrow gauge banana train was waiting for us. The old freight train had been retrofitted with seats. There was no air-conditioning but the windows were open letting in a gentle sea breeze. Tim, Jason, Monica, Rhonda, Jackson, and I took seats in the middle car. Slowly the train moved along the tracks and we left the jungle area and traveled along the coast. Mile after mile of deserted beaches with here and there a shack or two. We stopped a few times for photos, and then the train headed back into the jungle. Each car had a guide, and he pointed out wildlife as we passed by. Whenever there was a sighting by one of the guides they radioed to the engineer, and the train stopped so we could climb out and get pictures. There were monkeys, sloths, bats, and all types of colorful birds.

At the end of the line was another bus waiting for us, and it took us to the Tortuguero Canal where we boarded narrow boats and cruised up and down the canal. The overhanging trees provided sightings of birds, sloths, iguanas, lizards, monkeys, not to mention the beautiful scenery of the canal itself. All too soon the boat ride was over, and we were back on the bus headed for a banana plantation.

From the bus we could see acres and acres of banana plants and the little blue plastic bags that covered the banana bunches on the plants. We got off the bus and had a tour of the banana packing plant.

"I'll never look at bananas again the same way," said Rhonda as she watched the workers wash, sort, and pack the fruit. "I had no idea the harvest was so intensive."

"Me either," agreed Monica as she snapped some photos of the worker in the plant.

"At least there are no walls, so the workers get plenty of fresh air," said Tim.

"The whole culture here," added Jason, "seems to live outside in the open air."

"Did you see the schools?" I asked. "Open to the air. I'd love to teach like that."

"We're from New England," said Jackson. "We live our lives inside. More's the pity."

"This is our last stop," I sighed. "Then we have just three sea days before we're back in Boston and the cold."

"Cheer up," said Tim. "It's almost March."

"If winter comes, can spring be far behind," quoted Rhonda.

"That's Shelley's 'Ode to the West Wind'," I said. "Always the English teacher."

"Looks like it's time to get back on the bus," said Tim.

**

FBI agent Samuel Monahan, along with Pierre Hudon, were waiting for us in the security office. Tim and I had received the request to meet with them when our tour returned to the ship.

"I understand you have a theory about the jumper Jeff Donovan," said Monahan as he took out his notebook.

"I think you'll find it very plausible," said Tim.

"Go ahead then."

"Let's look at the facts of the case," I said. "Jeff Donovan goes to the bow of the ship when it's dark. The bow cameras are unable to pick up anything because it's dark. It's the only place on the ship that is kept dark so the crew can see clearly from the bridge. Donovan is wearing a backpack. Why have a backpack if you are going to commit suicide? "

"Why indeed," agreed Hudon.

"No backpack was found," added Tim.

"It could have been filled with rocks," put in Monahan.

"I don't think you can find any rocks on board a cruise ship," I said. "We also have to look at Donovan himself. He has been accused of stealing funds from his financial clients and faces a long jail term. He also took out a huge insurance policy with his wife as beneficiary. And in his will he leaves money to the Westminster Spiritualist Church. The leader of the church is murdered. Something is going on."

"All reasons for suicide," said Monahan.

"Except," I added. "Donovan made reservations at a small hotel in Aruba. If you are going to plan out your suicide, I don't think you'd be making hotel reservations."

"Maybe he and his wife were planning a date," offered Hudon.

"Except," said Tim. "He booked a single room for himself only."

"What is the name of the hotel?" asked Monahan. I told him and he wrote it down.

"The final piece of evidence comes from Ben, the cabin steward. Mr. Donovan brought a wet suit with him on the cruise, part of the snorkel gear. When Ben helped the wife move the Donovan's belongings to a new cabin, there was no wet suit. And there was a missing life jacket from the cabin.

"But it would be too far for anyone to snorkel to Aruba from where he jumped off the ship," said Hudon.

"When Tim and I were out on our balcony after he was reported missing, we saw several large ships had come to help with the search. Among the ships was one small yacht. What was it doing out there?"

"I think," said Monahan as he closed his notebook. "we need to interview Mrs. Donovan again."

"Do you mind if we tag along?" I asked.

"Not at all." he replied.

**

A look of panic crossed Julie Donovan's face when she opened the cabin door and found the four of us waiting for her. Monahan introduced himself as an FBI agent.

"Oh, no," she cried. "You found his body didn't you?"

"No, Mrs. Donovan," replied Monahan. "We just have some more questions for you."

"I've told everyone all I know."

"Where is your husband's wet suit?" asked Monahan.

"It's in his sport's bag. We hung it up in the closet on the first day but it took up too much room so we packed it up again.

"Could you show it to us?" I asked.

"Of course." She pulled a large sports bag out from under the bed, placed it on the bed and unzipped it. "That's funny; it's not here."

"Do you know why your husband reserved a room in Aruba?" Tim asked.

"There must be some mistake. We weren't planning to stay in Aruba. The ship wasn't staying overnight in Aruba."

"So you have no idea why your husband reserved a hotel room?" asked Monahan.

"It doesn't make sense. Why would he do that?" she asked looking completely confused.

"We suspect that your husband staged an elaborate ruse to make it look like suicide. We think he's still alive."

"Oh my God! I don't understand." Tears were running down her face. "Why would he do that?"

"He was going to go to trial for embezzlement and fraud," said Tim. "It was a way out."

"He did plan to take care of you," I said trying to soften the blow. "He took out a huge insurance policy with you as the beneficiary."

"Will you be able to find him?" she asked Monahan.

"Oh, yes," said Monahan. "The FBI will find him."

"What will happen to him?" she asked becoming alarmed.

"I'm sure he'll be looking at jail time," replied Monahan.

Chapter 23

Billy Simpson and I were out on the promenade deck watching the ship pull away from the Costa Rican port. The sun was warm on my face, and I was a little bit sad to be leaving the warm weather and heading back north.

"I've hardly seen you this trip," I said. "You've been so busy working. The excursions are over now aren't they?"

"No, there's one more excursion. It's a tour of Boston for those who are flying out later. Now we're gearing up for the next cruise. We have to process the paper work for those passengers on the next cruise who have booked there excursions online."

"How long is your tour of duty? We'll miss you at home."

"Parker and I signed on for six months; then we have three months off before the next engagement. So we'll be home for the end of summer."

"I can't wait for summer," I said. "Though this has been a great winter break."

"So you solved the mystery of the jumper?"

"We think so. FBI agents are looking for him now. They promised to let us know if they find him."

Suddenly Billy wrapped his arms around me and gave me a big bear hug before stepping back. "What's that for?" I asked.

"That's for being who you are. When you came back to Bath five years ago, everything changed. None of us would be here the way we are. We'd all be stuck back the way we were."

"Actually we have Rhonda to thank for that. If Rhonda hadn't bought the Erebus gift shop on a whim, I'd never have thought to move back here."

"No, I think you were destined to come back to Bath. If it hadn't been because of Rhonda you would have found your own way back to us somehow."

I was about to protest, but suddenly I had the feeling that Billy was right. Coming home to Bath was my destiny.

"There you two are," said Tim as he and Jason joined us at the railing. "Just look at that sunset." The sun was indeed a beautiful orange color as it began to sink into the horizon.

"Look at us," said Jason. The boys of Morse High's class of…"

"Don't say it," I said. "Let's pretend we're still young."

"We are young," said Billy. "We'll always be those boys sitting on the steps of the high school looking ahead to the future with hope."

"Where are the others?" I asked.

"Jackson is taking a nap, and Rhonda and Monica went to the spa," said Jason. "Parker, of course, is helping sail the ship."

"I think the Morse High boys of the class of nineteen-something deserve a beer," I said and then regretted it when I looked at Billy.

"Don't look like that, Jesse," said Billy taking my arm as we walked away. "They have non-alcoholic beer on board. It's my baggage to carry, not yours."

O'Brien's pub was crowded but we were able to find a table for four. The server brought us our beers and a container of nuts. A guitar player was strumming the strings providing background music to the patrons.

"Four more days at sea. I want to savor every minute," said Jason.

"Me, too," I agreed, "Though I'm anxious to see Jay and Argus and looking forward to getting back in the kitchen."

"And getting back to the agency," added Tim. "Who knows what cases lie in our future?"

"We have some cases here to help solve," I reminded him.

"How is that going," asked Billy.

"We need to find out who killed Nancy Gilliam and what the connection is between the Westminster Spiritualist Church and Jeff Donovan," I explained.

"What connection?" asked Billy. "I haven't kept up with your adventures."

"Jeff Donovan left his money to the church, or at least what was left of his money."

"Why?" asked Jason.

"The church invested their money in Donovan's company," I clarified. "I think maybe Donovan had an attack of conscience and wanted to make amends."

"What about his other clients?" asked Billy.

"As far as I can tell," added Tim. "the other clients were all big corporations. I don't think anyone will be sorry for them."

"But is there a connection with the murder?" asked Jason.

"That," answered Tim, "is something we need to figure out."

"And we only have three days to figure it out," I added. "And Monica and I suspect that the assistant minister who's now running the spirit circle on board here is a fraud."

"Why do you think that?" asked Billy.

"He was a magician; so he is skilled in illusion. And any magician can pretty much fool a room full of people. The spirit circles will resume on the next sea day, which is tomorrow."

"And you're planning to go?" asked Jason.

"Oh, yes. I am definitely planning to go." Suddenly I had chills, and I felt intuitively that I was on to something.

**

It was time to call my parents and confront them about what had happened at Lilydale to turn them off from spiritualism. Bonny and Clyde, as my friends had dubbed them back in high school, had retired to Florida years ago and showed little interest in coming back to Maine, though when they found out they had a grown grandson, they couldn't get up to visit fast enough, I looked at my phone, sighed and dialed the number.

"Jesse, are you okay?" asked my mother. "The ship isn't on fire is it?"

"Of course not."

"Well you never know. Look at that cruise ship in Italy. It sank."

"The ship is not going to sink. How's dad?"

"You know your father, crazy as a coot."

"You're the crazy one," I heard my father yell in the background.

"Quiet, you fool," yelled my mother back at him. "He's on the ship and it's on fire."

"Tell him to get off the ship," my father yelled.

"It's not on fire," I yelled into the phone. "There's no fire."

"That's nice," said my mother. "You must be freezing out at sea."

"It's eighty degrees here in the Caribbean, mother."

"Well dress warm, you don't want to catch cold."

In my head I was screaming. "Put dad on the phone please."

"I'm about ready to put your mother in a home," said my father taking the phone.

"That's nice," I said. "I need to ask you something."

"Sure, how much do you need?"

"How much what?" I asked.

"Money, of course. How much money do you need?"

"I don't need any money, dad. I'm doing fine."

"They must be paying teachers more in Maine than they do here in Florida."

"Dad, I retired five years ago."

"Then why do you need money?"

"Listen to me carefully," I said grinding my teeth. "I don't need money. I wanted to ask you what happened back in Lilydale that turned you off from spiritualism. You and Uncle Joe got upset with grandma and grandpa and never went to Lilydale again. And you both discouraged me and Monica from studying spiritualism."

"But you both did anyway, didn't you?"

"Yes, we did." At least he was sounding more with-it now. "The house next to your grandparents' cottage was being renovated. When they tore down the walls they found wires and levers. The whole thing was a fake."

"That's it?" I asked. "One house was rigged and so you thought the whole idea of spiritualism was fake?"

"We might have over reacted."

"You think? Have you called your grandson?" I asked to change the subject.

"Your mother just got off the phone with him. He's enjoying that dog of yours. I think he may get one of his own."

"I have to go." I said and then added, "Are you coming up to Maine this summer?"

"Yes, if your mother doesn't totally lose her mind."

"I'm not the crazy one," she yelled in the background."

"Love you both, got to go," I said and hung up before I had a desire to jump off the ship into the sweet waters of oblivion.

**

"That's the story," I told Monica. "That's why they never went back to Lilydale." We were sitting in the atrium bar sipping on cosmopolitans waiting for the rest of the crew to show up for dinner.

"How are they?"

"Crazy, but harmless. At least so far."

"There you are," said Rhonda. She was dressed in a long red gown with silver sequins and a red feather boa. Jackson, by contrast, was dressed in simple slacks and a plain blue short-sleeve shirt. The only concession to vacation mode was the sandals he wore. "I'm starving and I want cake!"

"Of course you do," I said. Rhonda always wants cake.

"Cosmos?" asked Tim as he appeared as if out of nowhere. His slightly curly hair was wet from just getting out of the shower. "I need one of those."

I saw Jason heading over to us. He is hard to miss with his height. He pulled up a chair from a nearby table and joined us. The server hurried over and took our orders. I ordered another cosmopolitan, just to calm my nerves.

"How are your parents?" asked Tim. I just shook my head. "That good, huh?"

"Are Billy and Parker coming?" asked Jackson.

"I think they'll meet us in the dining room," I answered.

"Didn't you just love Costa Rica?" asked Rhonda. "I want to go back."

"It's hard to believe that just this morning we were sailing along the beaches on a banana train," said Tim.

"It's been a long day for sure," agreed Jason.

"Now," said Tim, "we have three relaxing sea days before we head home."

I wasn't at all sure the next three days would be relaxing.

Surprisingly dinner was uneventful. Billy and Parker were able to join us so we had a table for eight in the ship's premier steak house restaurant. There was an extra charge but the service and food we received was well worth the cover charge. Parker and Billy kept us entertained with stories of behind the scenes events on a cruise ship. Parker's favorite story was the man who packed all his clothing into his suitcase and left it outside on the last night of the cruise, forgetting that he had nothing to wear on disembarkation.

"We had to give him a sheet to create a makeshift toga so we could get him off the ship," related Parker with a laugh.

"And we had a woman on the Aruba beach excursion who lost her bathing suit top in the water," said Billy. "She flailed around in the water and then decided to just walk out of the water like she had planned the whole thing. You could really tell the Europeans from the Americans. The Europeans thought nothing of it. The Americans, by contrast, looked with their mouths open."

My eyes welled up with tears as I thought about how much I love these people.

"Are you okay?" asked Tim.

"Just some dust in my eyes."

Chapter 24

It was early when I woke up. I showered and got dressed while Tim was sound asleep. Tim has the annoying habit of being able to sleep anywhere and also able to go to sleep as soon as his head hits the pillow. I, on the other hand, am a poor sleeper and lucky if I can get six hours in a night.

Out on the upper deck I walked the exercise track around the ship. There were other early birds out walking, too. It was great enjoying the fresh warm air. I knew by tomorrow that the air would be cooler as we headed slowly back to winter. I took the stairs down one deck to the buffet and grabbed a cup of coffee. Looking around I spied Monica sitting by one of the large floor to ceiling windows.

"I see you're up early, too," I said as I sat down.

"It's a family curse not being able to sleep."

"I keep thinking about the spirit circle planned for this afternoon. I think we have to expose Jerry Callahan."

"Yes, but if he is an experienced magician, he may be too sophisticated for us to uncover."

"I know; that's bothering me, too."

"Isn't that Rhonda standing over by the coffee urn?"

"It can't be. She would never be up this early." We waved when she turned around. She frowned until she saw who we were. She was wearing a pink workout suit with rhinestones.

"I've never seen you up this early," said Monica as Rhonda sat down.

"I woke up and couldn't go back to sleep. What are you two up to?"

"We've been talking about the spirit circle," I said and then went on to tell her what we've learned about Callahan.

"He's going to be careful with us because he knows who we are," added Monica.

"But he doesn't know who I am," said Rhonda. "I can go and pretend I'm looking to hear from my poor dead husband Ralph. I hate that someone is profiting off the grief of others."

"Not to mention the fact that he's casting doubt on the whole spiritualist movement," I said and they both looked at me. "I know, I know. I don't really believe in it either. It's just that I don't disbelieve in it really. I think there may be something beyond our five senses, but maybe not either."

"I think," said Monica, "that what you are trying to say is that you are a seeker of truth. There's a difference between a believer and a seeker."

"I think that is about right," I agreed.

"Well," said Rhonda. "I'm a seeker of good food. Let's get in the buffet line before all these old people eat it all."

**

The security office was a beehive of activity. There were laptops everywhere and frustrated looks on the faces of the security team. "What's going on?" I asked.

"Well," said Pierre Hudon, "we still have a murder to solve and the FBI is positive that the killer must still be on board."

"Has anyone left the cruise since we sailed?"

"No, anyone who got off the ship at any of the ports returned to the ship."

"So you're looking at passenger records to see if anything stands out," said Tim. It wasn't really a question.

"You should also check the crew," I said. "I saw some leaving the ship with baggage."

"Yes, we changed out some crew members who are going off the ship. The ones from the Caribbean got off at Aruba. But that was before the murder. We're very careful with our vetting process for employees. Each one goes through a rigorous security screening."

"I see," I said though I had my doubts about how rigorous the screening process might be.

"Anything unusual about any of the passengers?" asked Tim.

"Not that we've found. We gave the FBI a list of the passengers for them to look at, but the information we have is really just name, address, passport number and emergency contact."

"That's not likely to be helpful," observed Tim.

"The murder victim was traveling alone," said Hudon. "The only one who was close to her was Jerry Callahan, but we can't connect him in any way to her murder."

"But you can't dismiss him either," I said. I had a sudden thought. "How about the show performers? They come aboard, do their show, and then leave at the next port for another ship, don't they?"

"We have a troupe of performers who are always on the ship, but yes, we do have some acts that go from ship to ship. Mr. Dexter is in charge of on board entertainment. By the way I liked your act."

"Thanks," I said, pleased that someone other than my friends commented on it.

"I think we need to pay Mr. Dexter a visit," said Tim.

"It does look that way."

**

I wasn't getting any gut feelings about this case. It was almost like my sixth sense had deserted me, if indeed a sixth sense is a real thing; I had my doubts. Sometimes I think sixth sense is nothing more than the subconscious mind taking in information, adding and subtracting behind the scenes as it were, and coming up with a "gut feeling." Other times I think it's something else entirely. Actually over thinking it was making me tired.

"What's on your mind?" asked Monica as we walked around the promenade deck getting some fresh air. I told her what I was thinking. "You are over thinking it. Does it matter?"

"Not really, I guess."

"So are you ready?"

"For the spirit circle? Oh, yes. I'm ready."

Interest in the spirit circle had increased since the last meeting and the group was moved to a larger venue, which in this case was the Windjammer Bar. At least I knew there would be some "spirits" present if not the supernatural ones. There was a group of about sixty gathered for the meeting, and I could tell by the nervous chatter that people were expectant. Exactly what they expected I didn't know. Since this was a bar people had seated themselves at the small tables spread around the room and the others were lined up at the bar.

"Word seems to have gotten around," said Monica as we took our seats in the back.

"I'm not sure they're going to get quite the show they were expecting," I added.

Jerry Callahan walked in surveyed the crowd and then stood at the front of the bar. "Welcome to the Westminster Spiritualist Church's Spirit Circle. Thank you all for coming, and I hope you receive comfort and assurance that life doesn't end in death. I'd like to start by having everyone close their eyes and take nine deep breaths; as you do so imagine that you are emptying your minds of all negative thoughts."

While everyone else had their eyes closed, I watched Callahan survey the room through my half closed eyes. He was clearly sizing up the room. I saw him look my way at Monica and me and saw him frown slightly. He'd be frowning a lot more when we got done with him.

"Someone here," he began. "has recently lost a father. I have a gentleman here with a full head of white hair." That was an easy guess. In a room full of middle and late middle age men and women it's very likely that someone lost a father."

"My father recently died and he had a full head of hair," said a sixty something man sitting at the bar. Monica rolled her eyes. I could tell she wanted to give Callahan a kick.

"He wants you to know he's happy on the other side."

"Is my mother with him?" the man asked.

"Yes, she is. She sends her love."

"I have a person here, the spirit doesn't seem to be coming in too clearly, but I'm seeing the letter J."

"My late husband Jim passed away last year," it was Rhonda. We hadn't seen her when we entered the bar.

"Jim's coming in clearer now. He wants you to know that he loves you and that he is happy on the other side."

"That's funny," said Rhonda. "He was a two-face, lying cheat when he was alive."

"People change on the other side," Callahan said. I could feel Monica about ready to explode. I put my hand over her hand to keep her from slapping the guy silly. "He says he has been learning lessons on the other side and wants to ask your forgiveness."

"I call bull shit!" yelled Monica standing to her full height and pointing at Jerry Callahan. "This man is a fraud. He worked as a magician making people believe he could read their minds. He can't. What he is doing here is called a cold reading. He gives some very general statements and waits for confirmation by the victims."

"I object," said Callahan. "What I do is real."

"Shut up Jerry. What you do is criminal. How many of you out there have paid this man for a private reading?" About five hands went up. "I suggest that you pay them back their money or security is going to throw you in the brig."

"You can't prove anything."

"Rhonda, do you have a husband who has passed?" asked Monica.

"No, I don't. This man is a fraud."

"I want my money back," said one of the women.

"Me, too," said another.

"I think you need to come with us, Mr. Callahan" said one of the men with a slight accent who flashed his security badge. "Anyone who has given this man money should file a report with security."

"Please everyone," I said standing up and going to the front of the room. "Stay a moment." People looked around and then sat back down. "My name is Jesse Ashworth and this is my cousin Monica Goulet. We are the great-great grandchildren of Sebastian Ashworth and the great grandchildren of Wilson Ashworth, one of the founders of modern spiritualism. I know this has been upsetting for you, but we take a dim view of people who make money off the grief of others."

"Please don't judge the whole movement," said Monica to the crowd, "by the actions of a few dishonest practitioners. "There are some truly honest mediums out there who believe in what they are doing. Whether people can really contact the dead or not is something you must decide for yourself. I'd like to invite you all back here tomorrow at this same time for an honest discussion about spiritualism. Again, we are sorry you had to witness this."

The crowd slowly began to wander off. I looked at Monica. "We're doing what tomorrow?"

"We're going to show then what real mediums can do," she said and marched off leaving my mouth hanging open.

Chapter 25

Brent Dexter was in the middle of rehearsal for the final night at sea when we entered the ship's large theater. "Tim, Jesse, what brings you here? Looking for more stage time?"

"Thanks," I said, "but that was a onetime deal. We want to ask you about the onboard entertainers."

"Sure. What do you want to know?"

"How many of the entertainers get off the ship after their performances?" asked Tim.

"I don't really know."

"You don't know?" I asked. "Aren't you in charge of entertainment?"

"Only the song and dance troupe. All the other acts are booked by the cruise director. My troupe stays on board for the whole cruise."

"I see," I said. My scalp was tingling which was a sign that I was on to something, but what I had no idea. "Well, thanks Mr. Dexter."

"Please call me Brent. As I've said before, it's been forty years or more."

"Thanks for reminding me, Brent."

Tim and I slipped through the door marked "Crew Only," as we fished out our security badges. This was a section of the ship that passengers never see. Tim and I headed down the I-95, which is the nickname of the large crew corridor that goes from one end of the ship to the other. This is the busiest place on a cruise ship with crew coming and going on their errands twenty-four-seven. We headed to the area of the crew cabins until we found the correct cabin. Bill Keene, the cruise director, was in his cabin when we caught up with him.

"Ah, our two rent-a-cops," he said with a smile. "What can I do for you?"

"For starters don't call us rent-a-cops," said Tim, who has no sense of humor when it comes to work. "We want to know what performers have come and gone while we've been on this cruise."

"Dexter's acting company stays on board for the whole cruise. The magic act comes on board at the beginning of the voyage and catches another cruise ship at the first port. The comedian comes aboard at the first port and leaves at the second port. Then the jazz band comes on board at the third port and stays until the end of the voyage."

"Is it the same schedule for every voyage?" I asked.

"No, not really. That is just how this voyage worked out."

"Could you give us a list of the entertainers?" asked Tim.

"All of them?"

"Yes, all of them."

**

"What are we going to do with the list?" I asked Tim.

"We'll have Jessica check their background."

"I think we're missing something."

"Of course we're missing something. Otherwise we would know who murdered Nancy Gilliam."

"No, I'm serious. Something isn't right. We are missing something. I just don't know what it is."

"Are you going twilight zone on me again?"

"Maybe," I answered. "I have a feeling we are going north when the right road is to the south."

"Can you be more specific?"

"I wish I could," I said.

**

I was standing on the aft of the ship on the promenade deck looking down at the wake of the ship and watching the ocean disappear. Today was cooler as we were heading north. We heard that at home there was a blizzard predicted, but it was hard to picture snow when we were off the coast of Florida and enjoying the sunshine.

"Don't jump!" said a laughing voice behind me. I turned around.

"Parker! I haven't seen you in a while."

"And I haven't seen you alone yet." He walked over to me and stood beside me as I looked out at the ocean. "It's wonderful, isn't it? Being on the ship?"

"Yes, it is," I said. Parker took me by the arm, turned me around and kissed me.

"Parker," I said, "what are you doing?"

"We have a history. You can't deny that."

"I'd never want to. But I'm too old for this much drama."

"I know," he sighed. "Me, too."

"We'll always have the summer of '05."

"Don't even go there or I'll have to haul you off to a broom closet and have my way with you."

"I might put up a fight if you do," I answered. "Though maybe not too much of one."

"You're a flirt," said Parker. "I'd like to..." fortunately his cell phone went off; he looked at the caller ID and took the call. It must have been important because he started talking, waved to me, and walked off.

"What the hell is wrong with me?" I asked aloud.

**

Rhonda was in the atrium listening to a jazz band when I found her. She was dressed in shorts and blue blouse with a matching headband. I sat down just as a Filipino bar boy went by. I signaled to him and ordered a cosmopolitan. Rhonda ordered one, too and neither of us spoke until the drinks arrived. I took one sip of the drink and relaxed.

"What's up?" asked Rhonda. "I know that look."

"I just ran into Parker Reed on deck."

"So?"

"We got to talking and he kissed me."

"And?"

"I sort of kissed him back."

"And?"

"I kind of liked it."

"And this is a surprise how?" she asked putting her drink down.

"What do you mean?"

"You two spent a whole summer together sailing along the Maine coast. You have a history. But this isn't about that is it?"

"What are you saying?"

"I'm saying if you were twenty you would think this was fun. But because you are…" here she paused looking for a word that wasn't a number, "…older, you think no one could possibly be attracted to you. You forget that Parker is older too. Hell, we all are. You need to get over this age problem you have. Yes, our grandparents were old when they were our age, but we're freaking Baby Boomers and we are rewriting the book! Now man up, Jesse."

"When did you get so smart?"

"When I turned sixty you asshole. Now how about another cosmopolitan?" she asked as she signaled the waiter.

**

There was a message on the phone when I went back to the cabin. It was Pierre Hudon asking Tim and me to come to the security office. I went looking for Tim and found him sunning himself by the pool. In spite of the cooler weather heading north there were quite a number of people sunning themselves. The pool deck was sheltered from the wind and the sun was very warm. Tim was stretched out on a lounge chair wearing just swim trunks and sunglasses, looking for all the world like a mature, though not old, movie star. He saw me and got up from the chair. As he did so I saw several female heads swivel around and admire the shape of his muscular body.

"What's up?" he asked.

"We're wanted in the security office."

"Okay, let's go." Tim grabbed a polo shirt out of his pool bag, and we headed to the crew area with our security tags. Stepping into the crew area was like stepping onto a different ship. Here there were no wooden floors or paneled walls. No crystal chandeliers or flower arrangements. Here there were bare light bulbs in wire cages and gray linoleum floors.

"You wanted to see us?" I asked Pierre when we entered the security office.

"I wanted to give you an update on Jeff Donovan. He was caught trying to leave the island of Aruba. He was arrested, and he'll be extradited to the United States."

"So we were right about his plan?" commented Tim.

"It wasn't a very good plan. Jumping off a ship isn't that easy and jumping from the front of the ship is very dangerous. If you can't swim away from the ship you could end up being chewed up by the propellers or hit by the stabilizers. He was picked up by the sail boat you saw, but he was in pretty rough shape. The FBI was able to trace him because he was treated at a hospital on Aruba, and we found him living on a sailboat, which by the way was one he bought with the money he stole."

"Did he say if his wife was involved?" I asked.

"He claims she didn't know about it."

"And the money he left to the Westminster Church?" I asked.

"And that," said Pierre Hudon, "is where the story gets interesting."

Chapter 26

Tim and I both looked at Hudon. "What do you mean by interesting?" I asked. I could tell he was enjoying the dramatic pause in his narrative.

"He's been funneling money into the church for months. It's a money laundering scheme."

"Money laundering," mused Tim. "That explains a lot."

"So the church is just a front?" I asked. I was getting very angry.

"It appears so," confirmed Hudon.

"I hate when people use spiritualism to perpetrate fraud. It makes me angry. Someone is going to pay," I was getting angrier by the minute.

"Well, it gives us a possible motive for murder," observed Tim.

"Maybe," I said. "Maybe not." I was getting a gut feeling that the answer wasn't so simple. But then again the simplest explanation is usually the right one.

Just then one of the security guards burst into the office. "We have a situation," he said to Hudon.

"What is it now?"

"One of the ship's paintings has gone missing."

"This cruise is cursed," sighed Hudon.

**

Back in our cabin we were taking a break and sitting out on the balcony watching the ocean slip away. I wasn't too worried as the ocean wasn't in short supply. Tim's cell phone rang, and he picked it up and started talking. Roaming fees are expensive so we try to limit our calls.

"It's your back-up boyfriend," said Tim as he handed me the phone.

"Who?" I asked confused. What the heck does back-up boyfriend mean?

"It's Hugh."

"Bonjour, Hugh," I said into the phone. Hugh Cartier is a Montreal police officer. We met several years back when I was taking a cooking class in Montreal and helped Hugh with an investigation. Tim calls him the brick house because of his powerful build and good looks. He's one of those guys that you look at and wonder what they look like naked. No matter how good your imagination is, the reality is much better. Maybe I've seen him naked on a few occasions. Don't judge me.

Tim and I have a condo in Montreal and so we see Hugh from time to time. Tim has made him promise to look after me when Tim's not around, and Hugh readily agreed to do that. I don't get it, though.

"Jesse, I just looked at the calendar and realized that I missed your birthday. Tim just told me that you're all on a cruise to celebrate. I've got a present for you," and then he went on to tell me what he planned. My face was flaming red when he finished.

"Nice talk," I said. Tim was laughing when he saw my red face.

"When are you guys coming up to Montreal?"

"We'll be up in April," I said. "I love the way spring unfolds up there."

"Well enjoy the sunshine. It's below freezing and icy up here."

I hung up and passed the phone to Tim. "Don't you ever get jealous?"

"Nope," he replied, "At the end of the day I know where you'll be."

"And that," I said, "will never change."

There was a knock on the door, and I went to answer it. It was Pierre Hudon. I wasn't surprised to see him there at all. "Come in," I said. "Let me guess, you need some help looking for the missing painting."

"How did you know?" I asked.

"Don't you have a security staff?" asked Tim coming into the cabin from the balcony.

"Listen," he said getting a bit defensive, "this is a new cruise ship and the crew is new, too. They've never worked together before this voyage and to tell the truth usually all they have to deal with are drunks and accidents and mostly they run the x-ray machines for the baggage, or they scan the passengers' cards as they enter and leave the ship. Watching you two has been an education for the staff."

"What do you need?" asked Tim.

"Another set of eyes, I bet," I said. Hudon just nodded.

"Okay," said Tim. "Show us the security footage."

"Come back to the security office whenever you get a chance," said Hudon and left the cabin.

"Seems to be an awful lot of crime on this ship," remarked Tim.

"The missing painting is just a diversion," I said. "We must be closing in on the killer."

"Where did that come from?" asked Tim.

"I don't know," I admitted. "It just popped into my head."

Tim shook his head and made the sign of the cross.

**

"Bastards!" hissed Monica when I told her that the Westminster Spiritualist Church was a money laundering operation. "That's almost as bad as bilking money out of the grief-stricken souls who go to them for comfort." We were sitting on the top deck bar looking down at the swimming pool; where Tim and Jason seemed to be playing a senior citizen version of marco polo.

"I'll bet drugs are involved somewhere, too," I added. "Honest money doesn't need to be laundered."

"Bastards," she said again.

"It's all connected somehow."

"So you think Jeff Donovan and Jerry Callahan worked together?"

"Both Donovan and Callahan have requested lawyers and neither is talking."

"But we can't finger Callahan for the murder?"

"No," I answered. "He has an alibi, and we have him on security tape at the time of the murder. He was in the pub and we have witnesses and video that proves that."

"You think Nancy Gilliam was involved in the money laundering?"

"No," I admitted. "I think she was genuine in her belief in spiritualism."

"Me, too," agreed Monica. "Though I don't think she was an especially good medium, but my gut tells me she was real."

"What the hell are those two doing?" I asked pointing down to the pool.

"Showing off." We watched as Tim and Jason got out of the pool.

"There's something hot about a wet, dripping man," I said.

"You got that right," said Monica. "No ESP needed to figure that out.

**

Tim and I walked down to the crew quarters and entered the security office. I was beginning to think that maybe they should issue us desks and chairs since we seemed to be frequent visitors.

"Over here," said Pierre as he waved us over to a video station. "This is the footage of the theft of the painting." We watch as a hooded figure went up to the painting and removed the screws holding it in place. The figure paused whenever someone walked by. The thief was dressed in a baggy sweat suit, and it was impossible to tell much about the figure. The time stamp on the video read 3: 22 am.

"Is the painting valuable?" I asked.

"Not really," replied Pierre. "A few hundred dollars."

"Then it was definitely done as a diversion," I looked at the screen. "So early in the morning when few people, including crew members, would be around."

"And that is either our killer," said Tim, "or an accomplice."

"We can't tell much by the video," sighed Pierre. "The person is about average height, but we can't even tell if it is male or female."

"Don't worry," I said. "We'll find out who committed the murder and took the painting." I just hoped I was right.

Chapter 27

Afternoons on a cruise ship are quiet. People have had lunch, completed their morning activities, and headed off somewhere for the afternoon. On warm, sunny days they head for the lounge chairs, on cooler days they find a quiet spot for reading, go off to the casino, or head for bingo. There are activities of interest for about everyone.

Monica and I headed off to the Navigator Conference Room where about twenty cruisers had gathered to hear our take on what had happened to Nancy Gilliam and Jerry Callahan.

"Thank you for coming," said Monica as she stood in front of the room. "I hope we can answer your questions." I took a seat nearby where I was able to look about the room.

"As you know Jerry Callahan is in custody for fraud. Ms. Gilliam is dead. I'm sorry this has happened. I know your intentions were to find some closure and peace with the death of your loved ones. But I'm afraid that this experience has been extremely hurtful."

A hand went up in the back of the room. An older lady stood up. "Did Mr. Callahan have anything to do with Ms. Gilliam's death?"

"He has an alibi for the time of death, so the authorities don't think so."

"But," said another women, "the things he told me were accurate."

"Mr. Callahan did what we call a cold reading. He gave a general statement and then went on to see if any of you picked up on it. As he proceeded you unwittingly gave him information that he could use to make him appear to be in contact with the dead."

"Well, now I feel like a fool," said the woman almost choking up with emotion.

"Don't feel bad," said Monica. "The man had years of practice. You were just the latest victim in a long line of victims." Monica went on to explain more about cold readings."

"Was Ms. Gilliam a fraud, too?" asked a man sitting in the front.

"We don't think so," I replied standing up. "We think she was sincere in her belief that she could talk to the dead. Whether she really could or not is another question."

"You two," said a woman who appeared to be in her eighties, "are from a spiritualist family. But you don't believe in spiritualism do you?"

"That's a fair question," replied Monica. "We think there has been too much fraud and deception and that clouds honest inquiry. We are cautious, but open minded. But I guess we would have to say that we are both skeptics."

"But how does real mediumship work?" asked the woman.

"It varies from medium to medium," replied Monica. "Some claim to see the dead or hear voices. I tend to doubt those experiences. Most mediums I've seen seem to clear their mind of extraneous thoughts and just communicate what images pop into their heads."

"You must have some experience," said another man. "Show us."

"When we were teenagers," explained Monica, "and studying with our grandmother, Jesse was the better."

"Show us, Jesse," said the man. Several other were nodding their heads in agreement.

"I'm really not comfortable…" I began.

"Jesse," said Monica in a tone I'd heard before. "This isn't about you."

"Fine," I said. "But there is no guarantee that what I see will have anything to do with anyone in this room or anything real."

"First," said Monica, "let's start with a meditation to set the right tone. Clear your minds and think positive thoughts."

"Remember," I warned, "this is just an experiment." I was going to read Monica the riot act later for putting me in this position.

"Let us clear our minds of all negative thoughts and expectations. Now imagine that you are surrounded and protected by a bubble of protective light. Imagine that the light is glowing. Now say to yourself only positive energy is allowed to be present with us."

I stood at the front of the room and cleared my mind. Slowly images began to form in my head. I tried not to think about them by only report the impressions I was getting.

"I have a little blond boy here and he says his name is Jimmy." Immediately I heard a loud sob come from a young woman sitting by the window. Everyone turned to look at her. "He wants his mommy to know that he is happy and safe and that papa is with him." What the hell was I doing?

"Did you lose a son?" I asked the woman.

"Yes, his name was Jimmy. Papa is the nickname of his grandfather who passed."

More images where coming to me. "I see some type of military insignia. Did you bring something of his?" She pulled out a small toy soldier out of her purse. I was fighting my desire to get freaked out.

"I'm seeing a field of red, which to me means blood. Did he pass from a blood disease?"

"Yes," said the woman in a shaky voice.

"He's sending you roses, which is a sign of love."

I looked about the room. "I'm getting the image of a calendar that says 1910 on it," I said. "And I'm seeing what looks like a Navy plane from World War II."

An older woman wearing a red hat looked startled. "My father was born in 1910, and he was a fighter pilot during the war."

"And your mother has passed also? Because your father said he was there to greet her when she passed." By now I gave up trying to rationalize what was happening and just decided to go with it.

"Who has the son who just graduated from college?" I asked the group. A man about my age raised his hand. "And your mother has passed?" He nodded. "She says she's very proud of her family and that she was present for both the graduation and the family cookout that afternoon."

"She always loved a cookout," he said.

I was feeling lightheaded and drained, and I went to sit down. Monica got up and took over. "I think this has tired Jesse out, so let's take a few minutes and discuss what happened here. Jesse did what many mediums claim to do, that is he reported the impressions he was getting. It's up to you to determine what happened here. Did we contact the dead? I don't know. There are probably lots of explanations about what happens at a reading. One possibility is that Jesse is able to read minds and that the images he was getting where from you. Some scientists believe that our brains are like radio receivers, and that they can tune into the energy around us. It's possible that Jesse is able to read body language and determine something for that. I do know one thing; nothing Jesse did here was to deceive."

"I believe that my son spoke to me," said the woman who had lost the child. "I prayed before I came this afternoon that I would be given a sign."

"The information was too detailed for you to have made it up," said a small elderly woman. "I've lived a long time and seen a lot of things, but I believe you contacted the dead."

I held up my hand. "I can tell you that I had no intention of doing this." Here I gave Monica the evil eye which she just ignored. "I think each of you has to decide for yourselves if the dead can communicate or not. I make no claims. All I can tell you is that I reported what I saw in my mind's eye. I have to say that I am still a skeptic, though maybe not as much as before."

Monica led us in a meditation to end the service and people slowly drifted out. When everyone had gone I turned to Monica. "You are in so much trouble."

"Nonsense," she said waving her hand like she was swatting at a fly. "We were meant to be here and do this. If nothing else we've managed to salvage some comfort for those people. Remember they witnessed a man they believed in and saw him taken away as a fraud. And a woman has been murdered."

"But we're free thinkers," I protested. "We don't really believe in supernatural happenings."

"Or are we hiding under that label because to admit that we have a developed sense of intuition would conflict with our view of reality?"

"You might have a point," I admitted.

"It's part of our heritage. We need to acknowledge it and move on. Today we came face to face with beliefs of our family over several generations. It's time we faced up to this. You and I both know that we use our sixth sense all the time. It doesn't mean that there are spooks and ghosts around us; it just means that we are able to interpret the world around us differently. Everyone has intuition, you know. We were just brought up to believe that it's a real thing. We did a service here, and now it's time to move on."

"You're right of course," I said seeing the sense of what she was saying

"But you saw something else didn't you?"

"Yes, I did. I know who killed Nancy Gilliam!"

Chapter 28

Monica just looked at me with wide eyes. "What do you mean you know who killed Nancy Gilliam?"

"It was one of those images I saw during the spirit circle," I said feeling somewhat foolish.

"Who was it?"

I told her and she looked shocked. "The problem is I can't connect the dots. There's no motive and no opportunity that I can discern. It makes no sense. In fact I don't even know if what I saw was real or just my imagination."

"Are you going to tell Tim?"

"And tell him I know who killed Nancy Gilliam because I had a vision but no evidence, and that I don't even know if I'm right or not?"

"I see your point," said Monica closing her eyes. She took several deep breaths and her eyes flew open. "But I think you're right. My intuition says you're right."

"It would be better if Tim remains open-minded. If I tell him who I suspect, he may just look at one possibility and miss some clues."

"Well since you can't connect person A to victim B, then I think you need to keep it to yourself. That doesn't mean you can't focus in on the killer. Let Tim search for clues and suspects."

"And there's always the possibility that I am completely wrong."

"That's true, but for what it's worth, I think you're right."

**

"How was your spirit circle?" asked Tim when we met for drinks later in the afternoon.

"Monica put me on the spot and told the others that I would be happy to show what a medium could do."

"And how did you do?"

I gave him the condensed version of the afternoon, leaving out, of course, the final vision of the murder. "I seemed to have hit upon several accurate details. Though I'm still not convinced that there is anything to it. The fact that people survive death and communicate seems pretty farfetched to me."

"Then how do you explain it?" asked Tim taking a sip of beer.

"It's just a mystery."

"So you can admit to mystery, but life after death is farfetched?"

"I don't know. This whole thing has knocked me for a loop. It's all been easy to explain away as the mysteries of the mind, at least until now. And for the record I do believe in life after death, at least sometimes. I'm just not sure the dead can communicate with the living."

"In other words you're confused."

"Exactly," I said finishing off my beer.

"Another round?" asked Tim holding up his empty glass.

"And that," I said, "I am absolutely sure about."

**

I had had just about enough of the spiritual crap and trying to reconcile my various thoughts on the subject. Now it was time to work in the real world and look for clues and connections. There were, however, certain things I was convinced about. I was convinced that the stolen painting would show up. It wasn't valuable and not worth stealing, and I believed it had been a diversion. I also believed that the figure we saw on the security camera was the killer, but we couldn't tell if it was male or female.

By now I had convinced myself that the whole spirit circle episode was a bunch of hooey, and that I better concentrate on finding real evidence. But still in the back of my mind...

"Hey, Jesse, what's up?" I was looking over the railing at the ocean as it slipped by when my thoughts were interrupted by Billy Simpson.

"Just thinking about going home," I lied. "It will be nice to be home."

"I know," he sighed. "I love it here, but I miss Bath. I'm just glad you guys are here now."

"How long are you going to be away?"

"Parker and I will be home for Labor Day, I think we can arrange it that we're cruising all winter and off for some of the summer."

"That would be ideal." I looked at Billy standing there looking fit and trim and happy. "Billy, I'm so proud of how you've turned out. You've really reinvented yourself."

"I was trapped in an unhappy marriage. If you hadn't exposed Becky for what she really is… well, I don't like to think about it."

"You would have figured it out eventually I believe. But I just happened to be in the right place at the right time. You did all the hard work."

"There you guys are," said Jason as he joined us at the railing. "Boy, it's getting cold out here."

"According to the news the whole east coast is caught in a polar vortex," said Billy.

"At least you'll be heading back into the warmth once the ship finishes this cruise," I added. "The rest of us will be huddled by the fire until spring."

"It's March. Once we get through that it's only a matter of weeks until spring," said Jason. "I wish the cruise was a few more days."

"We'll just have to come back and take another cruise," I suggested. I saw Tim heading toward us and I waved.

"What's going on?" he asked.

"Jason and I decided to take another cruise," I answered.

"Don't forget that the cruise line is going to give us a free cruise for helping security out." Tim leaned against the railing. "But it would be good if you could solve the murder."

"It seems impossible," I sighed. Even if I knew who murdered Nancy Gilliam, I had no idea why or how. And there was always the possibility that I had an over-active imagination.

On the far end of the deck I saw Pierre Hudon and several of his security officers look around. They spotted us and headed our way.

"This can't be good," said Jason as the men approached.

"If I could speak to Dr. Ashworth and Mr. Mallory alone, please," said Hudon. Jason and Billy excused themselves.

"What is it?" asked Tim.

"We've found the painting, or rather what is left of the painting," he said. "It was ripped apart and thrown into one of the crew closets."

"What do the security cameras around the area show?" asked Tim.

"That's the thing," explained Hudon. "We have the figure in a black sweat suit, but when we see the face he or she is wearing a mask. We've got nothing on the security cameras after the theft because someone spray painted the lenses."

"What?" I asked.

"We see the figure in black who takes out a spray can of paint and then sprays the camera lens."

"How many?" I asked.

"All the passageway cameras from the stairway where the painting was stolen, down the passageway to the theater."

"What's the time stamp for the time of the spray painting?" asked Tim.

"2:30 am."

"So there weren't a lot of people around, and he or she stray painted the cameras before the art theft. I suppose security isn't fully staffed at that hour," I remarked.

"No, just two guys in the office and two more on call."

"So where was the painting found?" asked Tim.

"A crew closet near the theater."

"Let's go have a look," suggested Tim.

We walked down to deck six. The missing painting had been replaced by a piece of art work from the ships art auction gallery. We stood on the stairway and looked at the area.

"The security camera is right there," said Hudon. "Why didn't the thief spray paint that one?"

"Because," I said, "they wanted you to see them do it."

"It was a risk," remarked Hudon, "We could have rushed down here and caught the person."

"Whoever did this," said Tim, "is someone who knows the locations of the cameras and knows that you have a skeleton crew on duty at three in the morning."

"You think it was a crew member?" asked one of Hudon's men.

"I don't think we can rule it out," said Tim.

"Then the murderer could be a crew member?"

"Yes, if the thief is also the murderer. We can't determine if the killer is alone or if he or she has an accomplice. Also it could be a frequent cruiser on this ship. Someone who over time has learned a great deal about the workings of the ship," I replied. "Could you get us a list of the passengers who have cruised more than once on this ship?"

"Yes," said Hudon. "But it should be a small list. This ship has only been in operation for less than a year."

"Still," agreed Tim, "it's something we need to look at."

Chapter 29

The fiery red sun was setting over the water as I stood on the cabin's balcony taking a photo. Sunrises and sunsets are beautiful over the water. The Maine coast mostly faces east, so sunrises are common, but only in a few areas can you see the sun set over the ocean. It was getting chilly, and I stepped inside the cabin and closed the sliding glass doors. "Are you enjoying yourself or not," asked Tim.

"I am. I love unraveling a mystery. But the whole spirit circle thing upset me."

"Why is that?"

"I've been trying to forget about the whole spiritualist thing my whole adult life. It just doesn't fit with who I am."

"But you faced up to it. Now you can let it go. It really doesn't matter what you believe or don't believe. Spiritualism is either real or it's not. Your belief has nothing to do with that."

"You're right as usual," I said and gave him a hug.

"Of course I'm right," he said. "I'm always right."

"As if! So what are your thoughts on the murder?" I asked.

"Someone had a reason for killing Nancy Gilliam because it's not likely that it was a random act of violence. Most likely this has something to do with the Westminster Spiritualist Church. The killer or killers is someone familiar with the workings of the ship. We know the church was used for money laundering, so most likely that played a part in the motive. And we know that the art theft was most likely a diversion."

A sudden thought occurred to me. "Do we have a complete list of Jeff Donovan's investors?"

"We have a list, but some of the investors affected by his scheme were invested with other investment companies that, in turn, invested with Donovan's company."

"Can we get a more extensive list?"

"We can try," said Tim as he picked up his cell phone and dialed Jessica back in Maine. He got her voice mail and left instructions on what he needed.

"I think," I said to Tim, "that we're going to see one name pop out at us pretty soon." I didn't tell him whose name it was likely to be. After all I could be wrong.

**

I needed some serious down time, so I grabbed my book and headed to the ship's library with its comfortable chairs. I planned on doing some serious reading this trip, but as it turned out I had more than enough to keep me busy. Just as I reached the library door I heard a voice.

"Hey Jesse, how's the vacation going?"

"Oh, Mr. Dexter... I mean Brent. Things are going well." Only a few people knew that Tim and I were security consultants.

"Let me buy you a drink."

"Sure," I answered. The book could wait. We walked up one deck to the Seafarer Bar and found two club chairs shaped like sea shells off in the corner. A waiter came by and took our drink order. "So," I asked, "what have you been up to since you left Morse High?"

"I was the chorus teacher at Morse for five years and then I had an offer to work in New York. It wasn't Broadway, but it was still a good gig. I even got to act on stage. I didn't get paid much, but I invested my money and was able to retire. A few years ago I got bored with retirement and applied to work for the cruise lines. There I met my wife on another ship. We transferred to this ship a few months ago."

"So you're really a newly-wed?"

"Yes, so tell me about what you have been up to. What about Tim and Billy and Jason?"

"We graduated from Morse and went our separate ways. I went off to college, and Tim went off to the service. Billy and Jason began working for the Bath Iron Works. I taught English in New Hampshire for thirty years and then moved back to Bath about five years ago. I had lost touch with everyone, but we reconnected like we had never been apart."

"Speak of the devil," said Brent. I looked up to see Tim enter the bar.

"There you are," he said to me as he sat down. The waiter brought our drinks, took Tim's order and brought Tim a beer.

"Jesse was just catching me up on the last thirty something years," said Brent.

"How did you get Jesse to perform?" asked Tim. "I've never seen him on stage before."

"I told him it would be a big surprise for you all. He had a great voice back in high school. I did need to audition him first to see if he still had it."

"Oh, he had it all right." Tim took a drink of his beer.

"I don't think anyone guessed that he wasn't part of the company," added Brent as he finished his vodka tonic. "Well, I should get going. I've scheduled a rehearsal for this afternoon." Brent excused himself and headed out to the theater.

"Were you looking for me?" I asked Tim when we were alone.

"Yes, Hudon gave me the passenger lists from the last few voyages. I thought we should look them over."

"Let's do it."

"They're back at the cabin."

"Okay, let's go."

Back in the cabin Tim and I sat on the sofa and went through the pile of papers. There were quite a few pages since each voyage could have as many as four thousand passengers, the ship had been in operation for at least seven months, and there was a new voyage each week.

"The single starred names are the passengers who belong to the Voyagers Club. They are passengers who have taken at least two cruises with the Cruise line," said Tim as he passed me a pile of papers. "The names with double stars are those who have sailed at least twice on this ship. We should probably concentrate on them."

"Most likely if a passenger is the murderer, then he or she would have to be very familiar with the ship and have been on more than one sailing."

"There are a lot of names with two stars," I remarked as I glanced through the pages.

"Parker told me that a lot of people take back to back cruises so they have a longer vacation. They don't even have to get off the ship."

I was concentrating on the double starred names on the pages and pages of the passenger manifesto, so I almost missed it. As I went through the list one name jumped out at me. I was looking at the maiden voyage of the Prince of Denmark when I saw the name. Another piece of the puzzle fell into place. I was getting warmer, but I still had no means or motive. All I had was another confirmation that I knew who killed Nancy Gilliam.

By the end we had a list of doubled starred names and no idea what to do with it. "The only thing I can think of," said Tim as he threw down the last of the papers, "is to see if any of these name appears on the investors list that Jessica and Derek are working on."

"What would we do without Black Broker?" I asked.

"We'd have to hire a computer wizard who could hack into data bases."

"That wouldn't be a bad thing necessarily," I said.

"No, it wouldn't, but it would be more expensive."

Tim picked up his cell phone. "No signal. I'm going out on the upper deck and see if I can call Jessica."

"Okay. I'm going to hang here and read for a while."

I looked at my watch to see what time it was. I took my cell phone and went out on the balcony. It was cool and windy. I dialed Derek Cooper's number. I expected to leave a voice mail, but Derek picked up on the second ring.

"Jesse, is everything okay?"

"Hi, Derek. Everything is fine. I need you to check up on something for me."

"Sure thing."

"I have a hunch about someone and I'd like you to do a background check." I gave him the name and spelled it out to him. "I haven't said anything to Tim yet, because at this point I have no evidence, and I don't want to taint the investigation with speculation. If my hunch is right we might have a killer."

"If this hunch proves to be true, you'll have enough to charge the person for murder?"

"No," I admitted. "I'll still have some loose ends to tie up." I hung up the phone and stepped back into the cabin just as Tim came through the door.

"I thought you were reading?"

"I needed some air," I said.

**

It had been a busy day if not in action then certainly in emotion and mental activity. I was looking forward to a relaxing dinner in the main dining room with my friends. We had been at sea for two days with no land in sight, and I was ready to go home. I missed my house; I missed cooking, and I missed Argus and Jay. We were into March now and even if the weather in Maine was terrible, which is pretty much a guarantee, I knew spring would come eventually.

The weather was cool but not too cold so I knew we were still near the gulf stream and its moderating climate, but at any time we could pass beyond it into the cold North Atlantic air.

Tim and I were the first to arrive. I wasn't sure if Parker and Billy could get away, but they came to the table just as we were getting seated. They were both strikingly handsome in their uniforms. Soon Jason and Monica came ambling into the dining room. They made an odd couple. He was tall and big boned, and she was small and thin, yet somehow they seemed to fit together comfortably. Rhonda and Jackson appeared. She was wearing a flaming red flapper dress right out of the 1920s complete with feathered headband. Rhonda's wardrobe always makes me smile.

"What are you smiling about?" asked Billy looking at me.

"All of you," I said. "Sitting here and looking at you all, I can't think of a time when I've been happier."

"Don't get all mushy," said Rhonda, though I knew she felt the same way by the tear that was forming at the corner of her eye.

Luckily the waiter appeared with our menus and a bottle of wine before we all got too emotional.

"Where did this come from?" asked Tim as the waiter uncorked the bottle.

"Compliments of the captain," said the waiter. He filled our glasses and took the bottle away.

"A toast," offered Jason. "To friends"

"To friends," we all said as we touched glasses.

Chapter 30

After dinner we all went our separate ways and decided to meet for the ten o'clock show at the theater. Brent Dexter had promised us an amazing Broadway review type show. Since Maine is far from Broadway I was glad for the opportunity for a live show.

I headed down to the casino to play some slot machines. I never expect to win big and I'm always amused by those who think they'll strike it rich. I play for fun and usually either break even or win enough for a drink or two. But of course as soon as I win an amount equal to my investment, I walk away.

Cruise ship casinos are the smokiest places on a ship. I rarely go to the casinos because of the heavy smoke, but this was a non-smoking night. Even so I could still smell the residual smoke.

I had just placed my money in a machine when my cell phone went off. By this point I had given up on worrying about roaming charges. I looked at the caller ID and saw that it was Derek Cooper calling me.

"Evening Derek."

"Hi, Jesse. I got the information you wanted."

"Anything interesting?" I asked.

"Oh, yes," said Derek. He gave me the information I needed and another piece of the puzzle fell into place.

"Thanks Derek. That's a big help. See you on Friday."

"Yes, we'll be there."

The show was crowded and we were lucky to all get seats together. The production company had gone all out on the show with elaborate sets and costumes. The music and dance numbers were great, but I wasn't sure exactly what the theme was supposed to be, as there seemed to be a variety of musical numbers. It was something I'd have to ask Brent Dexter at some point.

After the show everyone headed back to their cabin. I was too keyed up to sleep, so I suggested that Tim and I head up to the buffet for a late night snack.

"Something's up," said Tim when I loaded up my plate and sat down with him at a small table by the windows.

"I thought we could sit and go over the case."

"Of course you did," said Tim. "Which means you either have a gut feeling about the killer, or you've got a theory. I know you too well."

"In this case it's both a theory and a gut feeling."

"Okay, let's hear it."

"Okay, let's start with a look at the murder victim, Nancy Gilliam. What do we know about her?"

"She's thirty-six years old and considers herself a medium. She is the leader of the Westminster Spiritualist Church. Her assistant is Jerry Callahan. We know that her church was used for money laundering by Jeff Donovan, probably with the help of Callahan. She was murdered on the ship by person or persons unknown."

"The question," I added, "is whether or not she was involved in the money laundering."

"The fact that she was murdered makes me think she was."

"Unless," I countered. "she was murdered for another reason."

"I don't know about that," said Tim. "Or is it your gut feeling?"

"It doesn't matter right now. Let's think about motive."

"My theory," said Tim, "is that she found out about the money laundering and was going to the police."

"I agree, except for the fact that the two people involved with the laundering each have a solid alibi."

"They could have hired a hit man."

"They could, but I don't think they would choose a cruise ship to do it on as there is no escape."

"Good point."

"I think her murder had something to do with her being a medium."

"You might be on to something."

"But," I said, "I think there might be more to it than that."

"Okay Jesse, spill the beans. I know you know more than you are letting on."

I looked down at my unfinished plate of food and told him what I suspected.

"Can you prove it?" he asked.

"No," I admitted. "Not yet."

"But?"

"But I have a plan."

"Of course you do," said Tim sitting back in his chair and looking carefully at me. "You always have a plan."

**

I was up early to watch another morning sunrise from the balcony. I was bundled up in my winter coat as we were closer to Boston. Today was the final day of the cruise and tomorrow we would wake up as the ship sailed into Boston Harbor.

Tim was still sleeping and I needed coffee, so I threw on my sweat suit and headed up to the buffet. I looked around and spotted Rhonda wearing a yellow sequined track suit with a matching turban.

"How do you come up with your wardrobe choices?" I asked as I sat down with my coffee.

"You realize it's only six in the morning, don't you?"

"Too many years teaching and getting up early. We used to meet at school at six forty-five for coffee every day."

"Yes, I remember, though it seems so long ago."

"It was a lifetime ago," I said.

"So what have you planned for this last day at sea?"

"Nothing exciting. What did you think of last night's show?"

"I liked it, but it seemed a little disjointed, don't you think?"

"That was my take on it, too. I think I'll go find Mr. Dexter and say goodbye. He was a great music teacher, and he let me do that number on stage. It was worth it to see your faces."

"I bought the video."

"What video?"

"The photography shop is selling DVDs of the cruise and your performance is on it."

"Are you serious?"

"You'll see. I saw Tim buying a copy."

"Am I interrupting?" I looked up to see Monica.

"Of course not," I said. "Have a seat. You're up early."

"Last day of the cruise. I don't want to miss anything."

"Jason still asleep?"

"And snoring."

"They all snore," sniffed Rhonda as she sipped her coffee.

"I hate that the cruise is ending, but I'm glad to be going home," admitted Monica.

"I think we all have mixed feelings," I said. "But this was a working vacation for Tim and me."

"Did you solve the murder?" asked Rhonda.

"Since last night? No," I said, but Monica was giving me a look.

"Here come the men," said Rhonda as Tim, Jason, and Jackson headed to our table.

"Did you call each other?" asked Rhonda as they sat down.

"No," said Tim. "Great minds thing alike."

"Parker and Billy will join us tonight for dinner," said Jason. "He said for us to dress up." Jason and Tim exchanged a look that I couldn't decipher.

"That will be great," I remarked. "It's going to be the last time we'll all be together until those two come home on leave."

"This has been a remarkable trip," said Tim. "Even if we didn't solve the murder."

"The day is not over yet," I said as I finished my coffee. "Now who's going to go with me to the buffet?"

**

I packed up my belongings except for what I'd need for tomorrow. We were instructed to leave our bags outside our cabin before midnight, so that the crew could gather them and get them off the ship. Tomorrow was turn-around day and the crew had to get us all off the ship and get all of the new passengers and their luggage on the ship within hours.

Tim and I ordered room service for lunch and then took a much needed nap. Tomorrow was going to be a busy day. We had to get ourselves off the ship, take the subway to Boston's South Station, and then take the Down Easter train to Portland where we would pick up our cars and drive back home to Bath.

I woke up from my nap and saw that it was already three in the afternoon. I had napped for almost two hours. Tim was still asleep, so I left him a note, grabbed my cell phone, and headed to the public areas to take one last look at the ship.

As I passed O'Brien's Irish Pub I saw Brent Dexter sitting at the bar. I quickly got out my phone and typed out a text message. I opened one of the apps and put the phone back in my pocket.

"Hello, Brent," I said as I sat in on the stool beside him. "I wanted to say good bye before we disembarked.

"It's been good to see my old students. I'm thrilled that you still have a great voice."

"Thanks for letting me on stage," I replied. "That was fun, and the looks on my friends faces was worth everything."

"You actually did me a favor. I had two of my singers fighting for the part, and I wanted to send them a message that I was still in charge. You have no idea what it's like working with a bunch of divas."

"So do you stay on this ship?"

"Our production company will be on this ship for a few months, but each of the actors is on a different schedule, so we'll rotate talents to other ships."

"Including you?"

"Yes, I'll work for six months, then have two months off then rotate to another ship for another six months."

"Actually it sounds interesting. If I were younger, I'd love to be in the company. But I bet you have to be young to have the energy needed." As I looked around the bar, I saw that it was filling up. I recognized a lot of the faces.

"Yes, it does. By all rights I should be retired, but I lost most of my retirement in the recession."

"It wasn't just the recession was it? You made some bad investments, didn't you?"

"Yes, I suppose that's right." He looked startled when I mentioned that.

"What I don't understand," I said, "is why you killed Nancy Gilliam."

"What are you talking about?" he protested, but he looked frightened.

"You stole a knife from the galley, you went to Nancy Gilliam's cabin, and you stabbed her to death."

In that moment I saw Brent Dexter transform from a confident music director into an old man. He seemed to shrink in size and whither up. Tears ran down his face and a sob tore from his throat.

"It was an accident," he said between sobs.

"How was it an accident," I said loudly. "Did she accidentally fall on your knife? You'll need a better story than that."

"I joined the church several years ago. I had hoped to get in contact with my late wife, but it only happened once. When I saw that Nancy was on this cruise, I went to see her. I wanted her to contact my late wife. She had refused in the past saying that she couldn't contact her because her spirit had moved on to another realm. I didn't believe her. I'd seen her contact the spirits of other people's loved ones. I took the knife just to frighten her. She freaked out when I pulled out the knife and tried to get away. Somehow in the struggle she got stabbed.

"So this had nothing to do with you losing your life savings?"

"No, of course not. What has that to do with anything?"

"The Westminster Spiritualist Church was laundering money taken from retirement investments. Some of your money was invested with Jeff Donovan who was using the church to launder money. I thought that's why you killed Nancy Gilliam."

"No, I didn't even know about that."

I signaled to Pierre Hudon. He and two of his men came over. They had appeared at the bar as soon as I had messaged them from my phone.

"I think you should come with us and then tell the whole story from the beginning," I suggested. I believed he hadn't meant to kill Nancy Gilliam. At least that was my gut feeling. I called Tim and asked him to meet us in the security office.

**

We were in the large meeting room in the security office. Dexter sat on one side of the table. Tim and I sat on either side of him to support our old teacher. Hudon and two of his men sat on the other side.

"My first wife Brenda and I were very happy. You two might remember her. She taught home economics at Morse High for a few years," he said to Tim and me. We nodded. "She died of breast cancer about seven years ago. I started attending the Westminster Spiritualist Church, hoping I could contact her. One time after about a year I got a message from her. She said she was safe and happy, but that I should let her go. She said I needed to move on. That was the only message I got from her."

I looked across the table at Hudon and saw skepticism on his face. "I believe you," I said to him. What I really believed was that he believed that his wife spoke to him from the grave. I wasn't so sure.

"I finally moved on. I got a job with the cruise line and I met my second wife and married her. I just wanted to know if Brenda approved of what I was doing. I asked Nancy to contact her, but she refused. She said she couldn't reach Brenda; she said Brenda must have moved on to a different existence, whatever that means. I thought if I forced her, she could find Brenda. I was desperate. I threatened her with a knife, but we struggled and she got stabbed. I wish it had been me."

"How did you get her key card?" I asked.

"I stole a pass key from one of the room stewards. He was making up one of the other cabins. I opened her door, propped it open, and returned the pass key before the steward noticed it missing. Then I waited for her to return."

"And the knife?" asked Tim.

"I joined the kitchen tour. There were about thirty people on the tour and I just stepped into the line. I hadn't planned to steal a knife. I was just curious about the kitchen, but I saw the red handle and I grabbed it."

"You stole the painting and spray painted the cameras as a diversion, didn't you?" asked Hudon.

"I was going out of my mind with guilt and worry. I was afraid someone would find out about my involvement with the church. I didn't know what to do."

"Surprisingly," I said, "We didn't know about your relationship with Gilliam. I thought that you wanted revenge for your financial losses."

"So how did you know it was me?" Brent asked looking confused.

"Spirit showed me your picture," I said, not caring if anyone thought I was crazy.

**

Pierre Hudon looked over at us. His look was stern, but I did see some deeper emotion in his eyes that told me he believed Brent Dexter's confession.

"I'm afraid," said Hudon, "that I'm going to have to keep you under surveillance. I believe you might be a danger to yourself. Tomorrow when we arrive in Boston you'll have to be handed over to the FBI. You understand why, don't you?"

Brent Dexter nodded as the tears streamed down his face.

"For what it's worth," said Hudon, "I believe you."

Chapter 31

We dressed in formal wear as Parker had demanded for our last dinner together on the ship. The whole dining room was festive with flowers and candles. When we were escorted to our table by the head waiter there was a bottle of Champaign in a bucket of ice waiting for us.

"What's this?" I asked.

"Compliments of the captain. He's very grateful to have the murder solved," said the head waiter.

"Does everyone know?" I asked.

"The crew knows, and I would guess that some of the passengers as well."

Rhonda and Monica where bedecked in jewels I had never seen before. "Where did you get the bling?" I asked.

"We went shopping," said Rhonda.

"There was a sale," added Monica.

The waiter filled our glasses with Champaign, and we toasted to good friends, we toasted to good health, and we toasted to the coming spring. We had emptied the bottle and then the waiter appeared with a new bottle.

"You should solve murders more often," remarked Jason, "if Champaign is the reward."

"And a free cruise," added Tim.

"Nice for you guys," said Jackson.

"So how did you figure the murder out?" asked Rhonda.

"It took a while," I said. "At first we thought that Nancy Gilliam's murder had to do with the money laundering, but we couldn't tie Jeff Donovan or Jerry Callahan to the murder. We also couldn't prove that Nancy had any knowledge of the laundering. And I couldn't prove that she was a fake medium either. But still Tim and I figured that the murder was related to the money laundering."

"So how did you focus on Brent Dexter?" asked Jackson. The waiter came to take our orders for dinner. After he left I continued.

"Call it intuition if you want," I said. "But there was something about Brent Dexter that made me uncomfortable. I had Derek back at the office check out to see if Brent had any investments with Jeff Donovan. I learned that he lost his retirement in bad investments, and that his money was invested in Jeff Donovan's business. That was the smoking gun we needed, it just happened to be the wrong one."

"And Dexter had no idea about the connection with his lost investments and the church?" asked Jason.

"Apparently not," answered Tim

"But we still didn't have any evidence tying him to the murder," added Tim.

"I had a feeling that if I confronted him he might confess," I explained.

"And if he didn't?" asked Rhonda.

"Then we did our best in the face of no direct evidence."

Our dinner arrived and we all realized how hungry we were. By the time dessert was served we were running out of steam.

Suddenly the lights in the dining room dimmed and the band music changed tempo and volume. A group of tuxedo dressed waiters gathered on one side of the dining room carrying candles. They began heading our way. All eyes were following the waiters as they began to surround our table.

"What's going on?" I turned to ask Tim, but he was kneeling on the floor. I was about to ask him if he lost something when I saw the ring he was holding. Everyone in the dining room was quiet. All eyes were on us.

"Jesse Steven Ashworth. Five years ago the only things in my life were my daughter and my job. Then one day I walked up to a house on Sagamore Street and there you were. My life changed forever. You are my best friend, the companion of my youth, and the love of my life. Will you marry me?"

"Timothy Sean Mallory," I asked fighting back the tears forming in my eyes. "Do you believe in the power of love?"

"With all my heart."

"Then yes Tim, I will marry you."

For a few seconds there was complete silence and then the whole dining room broke out in cheers.

The End

Recipes from Jesse's Kitchen

Quick Chicken Pie

A hearty and flavorful meal that can be thrown together in a hurry.

1 1/2 cup of mixed peas and carrots
1 1/2 cup of cut up chicken
1 can of condensed cream of chicken soup
1 cup biscuit mix
1/2 cup milk
1 egg.

Heat oven to 400 degrees. Mix together soup, chicken and vegetables and place in the bottom of a large pie pan. Mix together egg, biscuit mix, and milk and pour over chicken mixture. Bake for about 30 minutes.

Tuna Wiggle

This is a emergency meal and a great one to have in your storm cupboard.

1 can of tuna
1 can of peas
1 can of condensed mushroom soup
1 teaspoon Worcestershire sauce

Mix all ingredients together and heat on top of the stove. If soup is too thick add milk . Pour warm mixture over crackers or toast.

Orange Ricotta Pan Cakes

Jesse and Tim love these pancakes that they get at Ruby's Diner

1 1/2 cups all-purpose flour
3 tablespoons sugar
1 1/2 teaspoons baking powder
1/2 teaspoon baking soda
1/4 teaspoon salt
1 large egg
1 cup ricotta cheese
3/4 cup milk
1/2 cup orange juice
1/4 cup butter, melted
1/2 teaspoon grated orange zest
1/2 teaspoon Vanilla extract

Mix together flour, sugar, baking powder, salt, and baking soda. Set aside.
In another bowl mix egg, milk, ricotta cheese, orange juice, and butter.
Mix dry and wet ingredients together. Pour pancakes into fry pan over medium heat.
Serve with maple syrup.

Baked Jacob Cattle Beans

*Jacob cattle beans can be found in some grocery stores
or they can be ordered online.*

2 cups dried Jacob Cattle beans
3 cup vegetable broth
1 onion
1/4 cup Ketchup
1/2 cup molasses
1/4 cup brown sugar
1 tablespoon Worcestershire sauce
1 tablespoon dry mustard
several strips green pepper
1 tablespoon salt

Soak beans overnight. Spray crock pot with vegetable
spray. Put bean in pot and cover with vegetable broth.
Chop onion and add to beans. Add the rest of the
ingredients and cook on low for eight hours or until beans
are tender. Remove green pepper strips before serving

Cranberry Muffins

This B&B recipe makes for a good breakfast treat.

2 cups flour
2 teaspoons baking powder
1/4 teaspoon salt
1 cup dried cranberries
1/4 cup orange juice
1/2 cup butter,
2/3 cup sugar, plus
2 large eggs,
1/2 cup milk

Preheat the oven to 375 degrees .
Simmer the cranberries and orange juice over medium
heat. Set aside until cool. Drain off any liquid . Spray a
12-muffin tin with baking spray. Mix flour, baking
powder, and salt set aside. Cream butter, and sugar until
fluffy. Add eggs and mix. Hand mix together all
ingredients except cranberries, but do not over mix. Fold
in berries. Place in muffin tray and bake for about 25
minutes.

Stephen E Stanley

Made in the USA
Lexington, KY
08 February 2017